D0627444

Books *by* GEORGE HARMON COXE

Murder with Pictures (1935)

The Barotique Mystery (1936)   *The Camera Clue* (1937)

Four Frightened Women (1939)

Murder for the Asking (1939)   *The Glass Triangle* (1939)

The Lady Is Afraid (1940)   *No Time to Kill* (1941)

Mrs. Murdock Takes a Case (1941)

Silent Are the Dead (1942)   *Assignment in Guiana* (1942)

The Charred Witness (1942)

Alias the Dead (1943)   *Murder for Two* (1943)

Murder in Havana (1943)   *The Groom Lay Dead* (1944)

The Jade Venus (1945)

Woman at Bay (1945)   *Dangerous Legacy* (1946)

The Fifth Key (1947)   *Fashioned for Murder* (1947)

Venturous Lady (1948)

The Hollow Needle (1948)   *Lady Killer* (1949)

Inland Passage (1949)   *Eye Witness* (1950)

The Frightened Fiancée (1950)   *The Widow Had a Gun* (1951)

The Man Who Died Twice (1951)

Never Bet Your Life (1952)   *The Crimson Clue* (1953)

Uninvited Guest (1953)   *Focus on Murder* (1954)

Death at the Isthmus (1954)   *Top Assignment* (1955)

Suddenly a Widow (1956)   *Man on a Rope* (1956)

Murder on Their Minds (1957) *One Minute Past Eight* (1957)

The Impetuous Mistress (1958)   *The Big Gamble* (1958)

Slack Tide (1959)   *Triple Exposure* (1959) CONTAINING

One Way Out (1960)   *The Glass Triangle, The Jade*

The Last Commandment (1960)   *Venus, & The Fifth Key*

Error of Judgment (1961)   *Moment of Violence* (1961)

The Man Who Died Too Soon (1962)

THESE ARE BORZOI BOOKS, PUBLISHED IN NEW YORK BY

ALFRED A. KNOPF

THE MAN WHO DIED TOO SOON

When Casey inherited photographer Johnny Keeler's lifetime collection of negatives he suspected there was going to be trouble. Keeler had been an avid pro with a penchant for catching the awkward moment, and in his files there were sure to be a few embarrassing photos, and possibly some dangerous ones.

What Casey hadn't bargained for was the kind of trouble the police call homicide. As it turned out, a lot of people wanted those negatives, and wanted them badly. Some gambled on money—big money—to do the trick; and one, at least, was ready to resort to murder.

But just why should so disparate a group as a Congressman, a broker, a District Attorney, a disreputable private eye, and Keeler's own daughter all so desperately want the films? Casey had to find the answer—and he had to find it quickly. Two men were dead; the squeeze was on *him* now. And all Casey knew for certain was that if he didn't give the negatives up it might cause more trouble than if he did!

Here is George Harmon Coxe at his best—which means, as Erle Stanley Gardner has said, "uniformly entertaining, gripping, and exciting." Guided by the dean of American mystery writers, this latest excursion into the world of crime guarantees the reader top-level storytelling every step of the way.

THE MAN WHO
DIED TOO SOON

George Harmon Coxe

ALFRED A. KNOPF · New York

1962

L. C. catalog card number: 61–17813

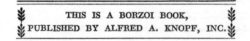

THIS IS A BORZOI BOOK,
PUBLISHED BY ALFRED A. KNOPF, INC.

FIRST EDITION

THE MAN WHO DIED
TOO SOON

For
KEN MARKS

1

TO ANYONE who knew him there was nothing unusual in the fact that Casey was the first man on the *Express* to hear about Johnny Keeler. Luck, as it had so often in the past, brought him to the studio—the accepted name for the photographic department—at the proper time, but luck had nothing to do with the telephone call that came to him instead of to the city desk.

Over the years he had acquired sources of information that were the envy of his colleagues on rival papers, and the flow of such information was a simple tribute to his character and personality. In the beginning he had cultivated these sources without regard to social, economic, or moral standards and the results were cumulative. He probably had more contacts than the mayor, whose tenure was limited by the whim of the voters, and if he had stopped to analyze the motivation which prompted people to call him he would have known that although some came as a result of past favors and others because they expected some potential reward, monetary or otherwise, the majority wanted nothing more than a simple word of appreciation or thanks. Often the tip was anonymous, but this time he knew the caller.

It had become something of a habit when he was out for the evening to stop by the office for a minute on his way home. On this particular Saturday night he had been to a hockey game where the Bruins had played to a disappointing tie, and he had hardly entered the studio when the telephone rang. The sound of it roused Cleary, who was alone and dozing in a chair, and he reached for it automatically as his glance focused on Casey.

He answered, saying: "Yeah . . . yeah," and handed the phone to Casey. "For you," he said, and yawned. "Some timing, hunh?"

The voice that came to Casey was quick and carried an undertone of excitement.

"Casey? This is Mort over on the desk at the Avon."

"Yes, Mort."

"It's about Johnny Keeler. I thought you'd want to know. Something must have happened upstairs—"

"What do you mean *must* have happened?" Casey demanded, instantly attentive now as he interrupted.

"A call just came from his room for a doctor and an ambulance. They said it was an emergency."

"Who said?"

"That friend of his—Mrs. Jensen. She'd only just gone up and—"

Again Casey cut him off. He said he was on his way and he was moving as he cradled the telephone, ignoring Cleary's request for information, not even stopping for a camera. Such a decision would have been unthinkable under ordinary circumstances, but Casey's mind was on Keeler and there was a good reason for the apparent neglect.

The call and its ambiguity worried him, but in the back of his head was the knowledge that at sixty-one—or was it sixty-two?—Johnny Keeler was the dean of the paper's photographers, and if a picture was called for, all the needed equipment could be found right in the three-room suite at the Avon which Keeler had occupied for more than twenty-five years.

Now, charging into the hall and seeing the elevator indicator pointing to the ground floor, Casey detoured to the stairs and went down in long uneven leaps, his coattails flying. His pace was unchecked as he sped past the startled operator in the small foyer, and then he was on the street and swinging left at the corner. Traffic was one-way here, but it was not heavy, and he angled swiftly through its flow toward the ancient six-story building in the middle of the block, aware that as yet there was no ambulance in sight.

Never a first-class hotel but with reasonable standards of respectability, the Avon over the years had deteriorated somewhat, both in its physical plant and in the clientele it attracted, until it was currently populated mostly by long-term tenants like Keeler, run-of-the-mill salesmen on limited expense accounts, and entertainers who could not yet afford better quarters.

The small and gloomy lobby was empty as Casey came off the street. Mort was leaning on the desk, an expectant expression on his round face, but Casey moved past without slowing down and their verbal exchange was short as he asked if there was any further word and Mort said no.

Once again Casey had to use the stairs, and when he came puffing into the third-floor corridor he knew why the elevator had not been available. Its door was open and the elderly operator's attention was directed elsewhere: he stood some distance away looking past another door into the room beyond.

There were three people in the living room of Keeler's suite and Casey identified them in his first glance. One—his name was Clem Alpert—was standing in the center of the room. A woman named Alma Jensen was kneeling by the third person, who was stretched out on the davenport, a thin, balding man with an angular, wrinkled face which never had much color and was now a shocking gray.

The woman, who was on her knees stroking Keeler's head, glanced around as Casey brushed past the elevator man. Her green eyes were wide open and frightened as she caught her breath. She seemed not to recognize Casey in that moment but said: "Oh—I thought you were—"

Her distress and disappointment stifled the sentence, and Casey knelt beside her and asked whom she had called.

"Dr. Russo."

"Yeah," Casey said. "He knows Johnny. If he said he'd come he'll be here."

He reached for Keeler's hand and was not sure he could find a pulse. The color in the thin cheeks scared him. The breathing made it worse because it was so strained and labored he was afraid it would stop altogether. The woman's tortured gaze came back to him. She asked if there wasn't something they could do. Should she put a pillow under his head or elevate his feet—

Casey shook his head when he saw that the collar and tie had been loosened.

"We'd better not move him at all," he said and then, to divert the woman's attention, he added: "What happened?"

Traces of shock still lingered in her eyes as she considered the question, and he rose and put his hands under her elbows. She came to her feet with him supporting her weight and stood motionless while he reached for a chair, a handsome woman of forty or so, big-boned but shapely, with a way of holding herself that did much to complement her figure. Her relationship with Keeler in recent years was well known, and for want of a better term she was accepted by those who were aware of the situation as Keeler's girl friend. Her presence here at such a time was perhaps unusual but not surprising. Casey eased her into the chair and told her to take it easy while he got her a drink. Again he repeated his question, and this time she answered.

"I don't know what happened," she said. "I walked in and Johnny was on the floor and he"—her glance moved to Alpert —"was trying to lift him."

Casey knew Clem Alpert to speak to, though they had never been friendly, and in that moment before the other replied it occurred to him that Alpert's presence here was even more surprising than the woman's.

"He just keeled over," Alpert said. "He'd asked me to get some ice and make a drink and I did. My back was turned when it happened. He didn't make a sound. He just went down—boom! He was on the floor when I turned around and I didn't know what the hell struck him. At first I thought he was dead. I tried to shake him and that didn't do any good. I mean, he didn't respond. I tried to lift him but he was all limp, and then she came in and gave me a hand."

Casey moved over to the cellaret which stood against one wall. On top of it was an aluminum tray with some melting ice, a bottle of bourbon, and two glasses, one nearly full. Opening the cupboard underneath, he found a bottle of brandy and poured some into a clean glass. He took it over to the woman and told her to sip it. When she continued to look at Keeler, he took her hand, wrapped it around the glass, and stood there until she obeyed his order. She looked up at him then, dry-eyed and pale. She was on her second sip when Dr. Russo hurried into the room, a chubby, bespectacled man who seemed always to be in a hurry.

He got out of his hat and coat while he questioned the woman. He opened his bag and took out a stethoscope. As he slid into the chair she had just vacated, Casey glanced away and let his eyes move slowly about the room.

He had been here many times over the years, but the place always looked the same. There was a comfortable, lived-in atmosphere to the rooms, but the furnishings would have filled any self-respecting interior decorator with anguish. Most of the pieces were heavy, and the style encompassed practically all periods in the past seventy-five years. Some of them had been supplied by the hotel when Keeler first moved in, but others had been acquired from time to time from secondhand stores and friends who were about to discard them for something better.

The bedroom was at the front, and Casey could see the old four poster through the open door from where he stood. This, the living room, had in addition to the worn davenport an old Morris chair, a club chair, a wing chair, and two or three occasional chairs. A battered Governor Winthrop desk occupied one corner, and a television set stood on a movable standard. At one time it had as its base an old-fashioned safe which looked like a two-foot cube mounted on wheels, but a year or so ago someone had come in and ruined it by knocking the combination off in an effort to open it.

The third room was Keeler's own idea. Originally a simple bedroom like the others, it had been reconstructed at his expense so that the one room was now two, with a compact kitchen on the left and a somewhat larger space on the right which had been converted into a complete darkroom. This had its own door and a solid, strong-looking lock. Now, aware that the door was open, Casey wondered about it. The door was usually kept locked except when Keeler was working there, and as Casey recalled this habit, his attention moved on to Clem Alpert, who now stood watching Dr. Russo, a drink in his hand.

A slender, sharp-featured man with small hooded eyes and straight black hair, Alpert had served some years on the police force before he became a private detective. His career had been undistinguished, and his last official assignment was the vice squad, where some irregularity—Casey did not know the details—had prompted him to resign rather than face a departmental trial. From personal experience Casey knew little about the man, but he had heard that Alpert's speciality was domestic problems of one kind or the other, his clientele jealous husbands and wives who for one reason or another were unhappy with their mates.

Considering this background now, Casey wondered again why Alpert happened to be here. It bothered him a bit, though he did not know why, but before he had a chance to dwell on the matter Dr. Russo got to his feet and just then two ambulance attendants arrived with a stretcher. As they gently transferred the limp figure, Alma Jensen turned to the doctor.

"What is it, doctor? His heart?"

"No." Russo closed his bag and spoke over his shoulder. "You can understand better if I call it a stroke, or a brain hemorrhage. It's not his first."

"But he never told me—"

"Didn't he ever have a sudden dizzy spell when he was with you?"

"Why—yes."

"Little strokes," Russo said. "During the past few years he had two or three cerebral vascular accidents that I know of. I told him what they meant and warned him to slow down.

He knew this could happen, but he didn't worry about dying, only about being paralyzed."

The woman had no defense against such a verdict. For a moment she stood there, a hopelessness showing in her eyes and her shoulders sagging. Then, seeing the white-jacketed attendants pick up the stretcher, she reached for the camel's hair coat she had discarded at the end of the davenport and slipped it on.

"I'm going with him."

"I'll be driving right along," Russo said.

"I want to ride with him. There's room, isn't there?"

"Sure there's room," Casey said. "Go ahead. I'll see that you get home."

Russo told the ambulance men to get Keeler into oxygen as soon as possible. He said he would telephone ahead so the hospital would be ready for them, and he was dialing as he spoke. When he finally hung up Casey touched his arm.

"Is it bad?"

"I'm afraid so," Russo said, and his expression was grave as he put on his hat and coat. "I've been afraid of this," he added. "We'll do what we can, but—"

He let a shrug complete the sentence and Casey, shaken inwardly by what had happened to his friend, forced his mind to work. He had not lost hope nor would he lose it while there was still a chance, but he understood that there were certain responsibilities that should be faced.

"Should I call Julius Levy?"

Dr. Russo considered the question before he replied. He knew that Levy was not only Johnny Keeler's attorney, adviser, and consultant, but a long-time personal friend.

"I think you'd better," he said. "And tell him to notify the daughter. She ought to know."

He went out quickly when he finished and Casey turned to Alpert, who had retrieved his topcoat and was adjusting his narrow-brimmed, pork-pie hat.

"How come you were here in the first place, Clem?"

Alpert's brows puckered and the small eyes showed quick resentment. "What do you mean by that?" he demanded.

"Do you want me to rephrase the question?"

"We were out together."

"Doing what?"

"That's none of your business, Casey."

Casey considered the reply and stood where he was, a burly, deep-chested man with a broad rugged face and a lot of brown hair, silvered some now and usually a bit shaggy above the ears and at the nape. His brows were strong above the dark eyes and nicks were visible in them here and there, reminders of small scars that had been put there in the past by some who resented having their pictures taken and others who, mistaking his basic good nature, had decided he could be pushed around. Now his eyes were more troubled than suspicious, and he was forced to accept the fact that if Alpert did not want to talk there was nothing he could do about it.

"Okay, you were out."

"That's right. He asked me up for a drink and I said sure."

"He was in the darkroom wasn't he?"

"For a while."

"Doing what?"

"How do I know? He didn't ask me in. He told me to go out in the kitchen and get some ice and make a drink." He turned away and went over to the door. "It's a tough break," he said. "He was a hell of a guy. I only wish there was something I could do to help him now."

He opened the door and went out and Casey stood where he was, his frown digging deeper, something telling him he had not heard all the truth and a sense of frustration nagging him because there was nothing he could do. He shrugged the mood aside as he remembered he had to call Julius Levy, but before he did he stepped to the doorway of the darkroom and snapped on the light. A quick glance at the interior reminded him to give the lawyer some additional information after he had broken the news about Keeler.

2

HE COULD HEAR the telephone ringing at the other end of the wire for quite a while before a sleepy voice answered. There was more interest after he had identified himself, and this was followed by a brief silence once he had spoken his piece.

"All right, Casey," Levy said finally. "I suppose I'm not surprised, but that doesn't help the shock much now. Yes, I'll telephone the daughter. Are you coming to the hospital?"

"I thought maybe you ought to come here first, Julius," Casey said.

"Why?"

"Johnny was in the darkroom before he had the stroke. You know how he felt about his equipment. All his cameras and lenses are there and I hate to leave the room that way. I mean open like that. Also the keys are in the new safe he put in. Aren't you his executor?"

"Yes." There was another silence. "Yes, I suppose you're right. Wait for me, will you? I won't be long."

When Casey finished with Levy he called the *Express* office and said what he had to say. There was still some ice in the aluminum tray and he found a clean glass and made himself a drink. He sampled it, took a big swallow, and put the bottle back in the cupboard. He took the tray and the dirty glasses into the kitchen, rinsed them, and turned them upside down on the drainboard. When he had dried his hands he got a cigarette going and moved back to the darkroom.

A tiny electric heater with a fan which Keeler sometimes used to dry negatives was on and Casey turned it off. A circular metal tank for developing thirty-five-millimeter films stood on the counter with its top off, and because he knew Johnny Keeler would not be using it for some time, he dumped

out the developer and rinsed the tank. At the far right, near
the heavy wooden cabinet Keeler had devised to hold his
equipment, was a camera Casey had never seen before. It was
a rapid-sequence model similar to one the *Express* owned and
kept available for any photographer who might need that
particular sort of camera. But there was a difference. The
company model had no provision for a flash unit and this
camera did. It had a strobe unit which was somehow synchro-
nized with the shutter, and although Casey had seen the
model advertised in trade papers, he had never actually handled one.

Once he had examined it, he moved to the other end of the
room and the small but solid-looking metal safe Keeler had
bought to replace the old-fashioned one that used to stand in
the living room. This had a key-type lock instead of a combination, and although the door was closed now, the key was in
the lock along with three or four other keys which were on
the same ring. He did not touch the keys nor open the door,
partly out of respect for Keeler's feeling—to some it would
seem almost a phobia—about having any outsider in the darkroom, and partly because he already knew what was in the
safe.

There were no stocks, bonds, or currency here. The safe had
been acquired for one purpose and contained treasures of another sort in the form of plates and films that Keeler had
saved over a period of forty years. These were the choice
items that he had collected and for the most part were important to no one but him. Once, in a moment of confidence,
he had shown Casey the two long metal boxes. The larger
one would accommodate negatives up to four-by-five, and the
other was a file of his thirty-five-millimeter and two-and-a-
quarter by two-and-a-quarter films.

The fact that the keys were still in the lock bothered Casey
in an odd way that he was unable to analyze. On the face of
it, Keeler must have intended to step from the darkroom for a
moment only and had been stricken before he could return. The only other answer that suggested itself, and this

was a little wild, was that Clem Alpert had taken the keys from Keeler's pocket while he was unconscious and had come in here on his own before Alma Jensen had arrived.

He did not like any part of that thought, and it was something of a relief when he heard the buzzer and strode forward to open the door and admit Julius Levy.

They went directly to the darkroom and Levy stood a moment in the doorway as his eyes inspected the interior. In spite of what must have been a hurried dressing, he looked very neat and tidy in his dark-gray topcoat and a gray Homburg, a small man in his early fifties, with lean and delicate features and a gentle manner. Thin-rimmed glasses magnified his brown eyes, and he had somehow a courteous, old-world air and a quiet way of speaking. When he had listened to what Casey had to say, he stepped over to the safe and tried the door.

"Did you look in here?"

"No."

"But you know what he kept there?" He watched Casey nod and said: "Only Johnny would know if anything is missing so we had better lock it up for now."

He nodded again when Casey told him about the rapid-sequence camera, and when he had found a key on the ring which fitted the cabinet, he opened the door and put the camera inside along with the others. When they stepped outside he found another key that fitted the lock on the door and he tried it to make sure it was secure when he closed the door.

"I'm glad you thought of this, Jack," he said. "When Johnny recovers consciousness he'll want to know that everything is locked up. . . . Will I see you at the hospital?"

Casey said yes and then, because the nagging thoughts inside him demanded some expression, he said: "Do you know why Clem Alpert should be here tonight?"

"No, I can't say that I do."

"Was he working on something with Johnny?"

This time Levy hesitated while his brown bespectacled

glance touched Casey and flicked away. "I'm afraid I have no definite answer for that either."

Casey sensed the evasion, but he tried once more.

"You haven't even got an idea, hunh?"

"Johnny discussed many things with me," Levy said in his quiet way. "He was a man of strong opinions, not all of which I shared. I might hazard a guess as to what he wanted to do tonight, but as his attorney I don't think it would be appropriate for me to discuss it. . . ."

Alma Jensen was sitting alone in a wicker chair in one corner of the second-floor waiting room when Casey and Levy arrived. She had not taken off her coat and her eyes remained fixed on something only she could see until they paused before her.

Casey asked if she had heard anything more and she shook her head. Levy did not stop but went over to the desk to make some inquiry, and Casey pulled a chair closer to the woman. He discarded his balmacaan and his brown felt hat in a third chair and took out cigarettes. When he offered them she looked at the pack as if she had never seen one before and again shook her head. In the lamplight her dark hair had a mahogany sheen which gave an added paleness to her cheeks, but her self-control was still good and there was no indication that tears had marred her complexion.

Levy remained at the desk and Casey sat smoking with his thoughts turned inward until, about five minutes later, the elevator doors opened and Dr. Russo stepped out with another doctor Casey did not know. As they spoke to Levy, Casey got up and so did Alma Jensen.

When they joined the trio at the desk Russo introduced the stranger as Dr. Twinning. The opinion he gave was discouraging. Reduced to the simplest terms, what Twinning said was that it would be something of a minor miracle if Keeler lived until daybreak. All signs indicated a brain hemorrhage, perhaps a massive one. They were doing what they could, but he was afraid it would not be enough.

Alma Jensen turned away before the verdict was finished. Casey heard a soft and tortured sob that she tried to stifle and he watched her stop a few feet away, her head bowed. The two doctors moved off and Casey felt a new emptiness inside him which he had no way to counteract. He swore quietly, under his breath and with vehemence, but that did not help. It was Levy who finally took command of the situation.

The expression on his delicate features could not mask the depths of his feelings, and though his tone seemed quieter than ever, his voice was even and controlled.

"There's nothing we can do now but wait and pray," he said, and indicated the woman. "Will you take her home?"

"Sure."

"Mrs. Jensen," Levy said as he stopped beside her. "I know how you must feel about this. I know how fond Johnny was of you. I hope you will understand when I say it might be best if you leave now. There's nothing more to be done here."

"Leave?" The word had a husky sound and her eyes opened wide to reflect surprise.

"I was able to reach Mrs. Garrett, his daughter," Levy said gently. "She's on her way here now. It might be easier for both of you if—"

"Oh," she said, interrupting as understanding came to her. "Yes. I'm sure you're right."

"Thank you. Casey will drive you home."

He turned away as he spoke. Casey waited until the woman had pulled her coat around her throat before he took her arm and went with her to the elevators. . . .

Once they were in his car with the motor on, the tubes of the police radio warmed. As Casey heard the voice of the dispatcher at headquarters, he leaned forward and snapped it off. He had two of these two-way radios in the sedan, put there by the courtesy of the *Express*. There were three regular station wagons similarly equipped for use by reporters and photographers as needed, but with Casey a different arrangement had been made. One radio, adjusted for the waveband of the *Express*, kept him in contact, when necessary, with the city room; the other was for police calls, and Casey ran the car on a mileage basis.

He belonged to the Guild like all the other newsmen and was theoretically limited to a certain number of hours a week before overtime was involved. But he kept no regular hours, the company leaving up to him how much time he put in; it was the same way with his mileage. When he was working the *Express* paid; when he was on his own the expense was his. Now, with both radios off, he had a private sedan, and the unnatural silence made him forget his companion for the moment and think of Keeler.

There were some who maintained, and not without justification, that Keeler was an eccentric. A few like McGrath, the managing editor, who thought all photographers were a little nuts anyway, maintained that Keeler was an unpredictable oddball. All admitted that he was an independent thinker who gave not a damn for the opinion of others and maintained an antipathy for a lot of conventions that most people held sacred. For all of this, he was generous, soft-hearted, immensely popular, and loyal to his friends.

He had been married for a while a long time ago, but the marriage had foundered after a few years, and Keeler was the first to admit it was mostly his fault. There had been a short honeymoon and when it was over he had installed his bride in the hotel apartment that even in those days was his home. He had tried to indoctrinate his wife into his way of life, since he knew no other, and for a while the arrangement seemed to work. He bought a car, but because he refused to learn to drive his wife was pressed into service as a part-time chauffeur. In those days, before the union, his hours were irregular and at times, when he was on a story, he would not be home for days. Even so, it took the birth of his daughter to make the break permanent.

As the child grew older, his wife rebelled at life at the Avon. When Keeler refused to move she had rented a small bungalow in one of the Newtons and moved out. This, apparently, was all right with Keeler. He mailed a monthly check for her support and continued to live his own life. He supplied the funds to send his daughter through college, but he'd had little success as a father. He remembered the girl's birthdays and did well by her at Christmas time, but his attempts to take her to dinner and the theater from time to time did little to break down the barriers which had been erected over the years.

He was fond of her in his way, but he seldom saw her. For her part, she lived in a world that was far removed from his. She'd been out of college only a few months before her mother died, and when she decided to marry a man named Stanley Garrett she did not discuss the matter with Keeler but simply called him up and told him what she was going to do. Keeler, knowing Garrett, had protested, but by then it was much too late for his opinion to influence her decision.

Such thoughts of the daughter had the effect of bringing Casey's mind back to the woman beside him, and as he again became aware of her he gave her a sidewise glance. She was sitting in her corner, her chin up now and her eyes fixed on the road ahead. Reflected light from the instrument panel was kind to her profile, and he was once more reminded that this was a handsome woman.

He understood that she was a widow, though he knew nothing about her past. He was not sure how Keeler had met her nor did he know when they began to go together. A partner in a small dress shop on Boylston Street, she was her own best advertisement, and it had been said that a small investment on Keeler's part had helped to establish the business. Others suggested that Keeler paid part or all the rent of the three-room apartment she maintained out beyond the medical school. How much of this was true, Casey did not know; what he did know was that since Keeler had been going with her he had seemed a happier and more contented man.

Whatever the arrangement, there was nothing clandestine about it. That they were seldom seen out together was due simply to the fact that Keeler hated to dine out and spent no time in night clubs. Over the years he had abused himself physically by driving himself too hard and drinking too much, though he was seldom drunk. His failure to get enough sleep and unwise eating habits had not helped, and it was Casey's thought that Keeler had reached an age where he not only needed but appreciated feminine companionship and the little attentions a woman could give.

He knew there were times when Keeler would leave the office on a Friday night and not come back until Monday morning; and from things that were said later he guessed that Keeler had spent the weekend quietly in that three-room apartment. He also knew that Alma Jensen seldom came to the Avon, and that made him wonder again about her appearance at the hotel earlier. There were a lot of things he wanted to say, but this was not the time so he put a mental limit on his questions.

"Alma."

He had stopped at a traffic light and he watched her as the word registered and she turned her head.

"Yes, Jack."

"Did you just *happen* to stop at Johnny's place when you did?"

The light changed and he accelerated the car. He was in high before she gave him her reply.

"Not exactly. He said he would be busy and wouldn't be out to the apartment. I asked him if it was all right if I stopped by for one drink. He said yes but he might not be back much before twelve and if he wasn't there I shouldn't wait."

"He didn't tell you what he was going to be doing?"

He was watching the car ahead now, not looking at her, and he was not sure she heard him. He was about ready to repeat the question when she replied.

"No."

"Did he tell you he'd be out with Clem Alpert?"

Again the pause.

"No."

"You didn't expect to find Alpert there?"

"No, certainly not." She answered more quickly this time,

and there was a new inflection in her voice as she changed the subject. "I'm sorry I have to be like this. I guess I'm a very selfish woman. I've been praying a little tonight, but mostly I've been too busy feeling sorry for myself to think about anything else."

The apartment house was just ahead and Casey pulled into the curb not far from the entrance. As he stopped and started to reach for the door, she leaned toward him and put her hand on his arm.

"Don't get out," she said. "Please."

"I was just going to the door—"

"Not even that. I want you to come and see me, and real soon. But right now I've got some crying to do and I'm not sure how long I can hold back."

She got out quickly and Casey watched her hurry to the glass door and step into the entryway. He saw her fumble in her bag for a key and open the inner door. As it swung behind her, he put the car in gear and when he got underway he began again to swear softly.

He wanted a drink now and he wanted it bad. He also knew there was only one place to get one. That was the trouble with this town. At midnight on Saturday they pulled in the sidewalks, and if you wanted to do any drinking you either did it with friends or at home. Right now he felt as if he had no friends, but there was plenty to drink in his apartment and he was in a hurry to get there.

3

CASEY SLEPT late, as he often did on Sunday mornings, and as he became aware of his surroundings he also became conscious of his hangover. He had had more to drink than usual, but it had seemed like the thing to do at the time and he did not regret it now.

A glance at his watch told him it was nearly ten and he rolled over on his side, propping his head on one hand and elbow while he considered the telephone on the bedside stand. Until recently he had used a homemade silencer to keep the phone from ringing when he did not want to be disturbed. This was nothing more than a piece of felt which he inserted in the bellbox, but the new instrument that had been installed had a gadget on it that adjusted the volume of the ring so that it would be loud or soft. An extra turn made it silent, and that's the way he had it now.

He gave the switch a turn before he dialed the *Express* number and asked for the city room, and the word that he had dreaded came to him when he asked his question. Johnny Keeler was gone and Dr. Twinning had been right and things were not going to be the same at the *Express*. He voiced such thoughts as quickly as he could and hung up after saying that he might stop by later in the day. Then he sat on the edge of the bed, a brooding, bearlike figure, his thick hair tousled and shaggy, his dark and melancholy gaze fixed sightlessly across the room.

It was a while before he could find the energy to put on his slippers, and then he shuffled into the living room and through the little hallway to the door. His copy of the *Express* was just outside and he brought it back to the bedroom, leafing through the main section until he found the short piece under the one-column head which said that a veteran newsman had been suddenly stricken in his hotel apartment. There would be more in the following editions, a lot more, and he carried that thought with him as he went into the kitchen and put the water on for his coffee. . . .

It was nearly four o'clock when Casey entered the *Express* building. He had kept to his apartment all day, making himself a good breakfast, cleaning up thoroughly, writing checks for old and new bills, working on his income tax, and reading the paper. Now, stepping into the elevator, and with no good reason in mind, he rode to the editorial floor instead of getting off at the studio. A working staff was there at that hour, but they were not too busy and everywhere he turned there was subdued and often nostalgic comment about Johnny Keeler. Three of the conversations Casey had were longer than usual, and he remembered them because of the familiar sidelights they shed on Keeler's character.

The first was with a veteran named Clancy. He had been with the paper nearly as long as Keeler and for some years now had been a fixture in the slot. Casey bumped into him at the soft-drink machine, and as they moved aside to repeat again the utterly sincere but hackneyed phrases that had been said before, Clancy recalled an evening he had spent in Keeler's suite a long time ago.

"Did you ever go to one of those Saturday night dos he'd have once in a while when he'd get some stripper to come over to his place and put on an act?" he asked.

"A couple of times," Casey said. "That was quite a while back."

"Sure. When they had burlesque at the Old Howard. He never seemed to have too much trouble getting some girl to come because he used to take publicity pictures for them. You know, the kind they stick out front in a club they're working at or give to a press agent. I understand those kind cost money, but Johnny would make the prints for free. Then, when he wanted some girl to come over and have a drink and do a little dance, the answer was usually yes. He knew a lot of the headliners and, what the hell, it was just a job with them."

"They always knew Johnny would keep things in line, too," Casey said.

"Oh, sure. Sure. What difference did it make to a stripper whether she was putting on an act for six guys or six hundred?" Clancy's eyes gleamed a little at the thought and he took another swallow from the bottle. "Two times I was there the girl went right down to the G-string. Why not? She was having a good time, too. And like you said, she knew the house rules."

He paused again, his tone reminiscent. "Johnny was a

stickler for keeping the party clean. No sex. No sir, not on those nights, anyway. Nobody went into the bedroom but the girl, and then only to put her clothes back on. Nobody made a pass. All you had to do was put your hand on one of those dancers and you were out in the hall on your butt. I've seen it happen. . . . And you know who got the biggest kick out of it?"

"Johnny."

"Yeah. Because he got to take some pictures. Not just because he had a practically naked woman for a model, either. He could have got that any time. But he'd keep popping away with those flashbulbs and drinking and chuckling, and he wouldn't be just watching the girl, either; he'd take pictures of everybody. I've seen some of them. They were a riot. Guys sitting around bug-eyed, me included. Then after the girl had her clothes on, she'd come out and have a drink with us and maybe a sandwich. Johnny'd make us kick in with something for the girl's time even when she protested. He'd tuck it in her purse and call a cab for her and send her back to her hotel. And you know something? Most of those girls were okay. Maybe some were tramps, but those I saw never got looped, never got out of line. They kidded around with you now and then for laughs, but that was all."

"They liked Johnny," Casey said.

"That's what I mean. They liked to get their picture taken and he liked to take them." He stopped to deposit the empty bottle in the case on the floor and arched his back. "It'll be a long time before you meet another guy like Johnny. He'll be missed. . . ."

The second remembrance of the past came from Tom Reese, a slender, graying man, bent-shouldered now from his years on rewrite and probably the only remaining desk man in town who still wore an eye shade. He was working on a crossword puzzle when Casey stopped in his idle tour of the city room, and as they said the things that had been said before, Reese took off the eye shade and leaned back.

"A great guy," he said, a faraway look touching his glance. "A little crazy, of course—I guess that's standard equipment for most of you camera characters—but who wouldn't be, living alone like that all those years at the Avon. Imagine not ever learning to drive a car."

"He didn't have to," Casey said. "If he couldn't con somebody in the office to drive him, he'd call a cab."

"But I mean, expecting his wife to do it after they were married. Did you know her?"

"Only by sight," Casey said. "She'd already left him when I came to work."

"She was a nice kid, but after the daughter came she just couldn't take it, and who could blame her? Johnny still wanted to do all the things he'd always done. Like those poker parties he'd have every two or three weeks. Did you ever sit in on one of those sessions?"

"Not often," Casey said. "I couldn't afford it in those days."

"They weren't that steep. Twenty-five and fifty."

"But with unlimited raises. You could blow a week's pay."

"Never more than six players," Reese continued as though he had not heard. "And nothing but straight five-card stud. It was prohibition then—I mean the time I'm talking about—and Johnny'd have some bathtub gin and ginger ale, and the kitty paid for the sandwiches we had sent up. From Saturday after work until Sunday evening was nothing, and when Johnny folded on a hand he'd be fooling with one of those cameras of his."

He grinned and said: "I never saw such a guy to take pictures. Of course, he probably lifted the films and stuff from the office, but he never seemed to get tired. You'd be trying to figure if a guy had drawn to a straight and a light would explode in your face. He got some good pictures, too. Candid stuff. Wonderful. Generous, too, about giving you a copy if you asked him, but funny about films. I asked once because I wanted to get some prints made, but no dice. I mean he wouldn't even listen. Why was that?"

Casey said he didn't know; it was just the way Keeler felt about his negatives.

"He was real bugged on the subject," Reese said. "Like it was some neurosis. Prints yes, negatives no."

"It was the way he was. Everyone has idiosyncrasies. That was one of Johnny's."

"I've had other fellows tell me it happened to them." Reese grunted softly and rubbed his eyes. "He must have taken a hundred thousand pictures, a lot of them on his own time. How many did he keep? . . . I heard he had a couple of boxes of negatives in his safe," he added, expecting no answer. "Probably the ones he happened to like best. The rest he destroyed. It's hard to understand why he was so unreasonable about that one subject, but I guess no one ever understands anyone else anyway. I mean not really. You're a photographer, but if you can't explain it, who can?"

"I've got some negatives of my own I'm pretty jealous of," Casey said as he slid his thigh off the corner of the desk. "Maybe I understand a little of what was in Johnny's mind. But putting the thought in specific terms is something else again. That's a job for you writers. . . ."

The third and last episode from the past that shed some light on another facet of Johnny Keeler's character was one that Casey had witnessed, at least in part. In his wanderings he had come finally to the studio, where he found Shelby and Lanvin sitting on opposite sides of his desk. There was a deck of cards between them, but they weren't in use at the moment. Shelby was laughing and Lanvin, who apparently had been telling a story, stopped when he saw Casey. Shelby, who had only been on the paper for a year, stood up to offer Casey his chair, and Lanvin said:

"I was telling him about the hamburgers and the ferrotyper."

Casey told Shelby to sit still. He said he wasn't going to stay, but he eased down in a nearby chair and stretched his legs.

"Did it really happen?" Shelby said, his eagerness showing in his young face and his eyes bright with interest.

"Sure it happened," Casey said.

"And you were here?"

"I was sitting right over there in the corner." Casey pointed, and as remembered things came back to him, the lines in his rugged face softened and a gleam of humor began to work at the corners of his dark eyes. "I'd finished my shift and had dinner, but I came back to kill a little time. There wasn't anybody else here and I was reading a magazine when Johnny came in."

"He was carrying a little load, wasn't he?" Lanvin said.

"He'd had a few," Casey admitted. "He came in, weaving a little, with this paper bag in his hand. He tossed his cap on the desk—"

"He wore a cap?" Shelby said.

"He did then. He saw me sitting there, but he didn't say anything and neither did I because I didn't know what kind of a mood he was in and sometimes he was a little touchy. He went right on by and made the turn"—Casey nodded toward the corridor which led to the printing room on the immediate left, and if one continued, to the darkroom cubicles—"and I thought maybe he had some work to do."

"You didn't wonder about the bag?" Shelby asked.

"Why should I? I thought he probably had a sandwich in there, but I didn't think anything of it. I went back to my magazine and a little later I thought I smelled something but I didn't think much about that either."

He paused, visualizing again the ferrotype machine they had had at the time. They came in various models. Some were flat, some were nearly vertical, and some were rounded. This one had a very slight tilt from the horizontal and was large enough to accommodate four eight-by-ten prints. In many ways it was not unlike an electric grill. It had heating coils and a rheostat to regulate the current, but its outstanding characteristic was a smooth, gleaming, highly polished metal surface which was essential to give a photograph its necessary gloss.

Its operation was simple enough. When the water had been squeezed from a print—the device in those days had not been too different from the rollers on an old-fashioned washing machine—the print was slapped face down on the warm metal. It could be left there safely while work continued, and when the print was dry it would buckle slightly and pop loose from the smooth surface and slide off of its own accord, to be caught by a rim at the bottom. . . .

"And what you smelled," Lanvin said, prompting him, "was hamburg cooking."

"Yeah," said Casey, and for the first time that day he grinned. "I don't know where he got it; he never told me. But I guess he was hungry and for some reason or other he did not want to stop in a restaurant, but he did stop somewhere to pick up two hamburg patties and two rolls."

Shelby started to snicker. He was trying to smother it so he would not interrupt the story, but the sound was infectious. Casey's grin had moved into his eyes now, and he said:

"The first thing I know, he marches out here with two hamburgers in his hand. He hands me one without a word, sits down, and begins to eat the other."

"How was it?" Lanvin said, beginning to do some chuckling of his own.

"Pretty good," Casey said. "Of course, he had to turn the heat up on the ferrotyper and he didn't have any grease so it was a little burned on the outside—"

He stopped, looked at the other two; then he, too, began to chuckle because somehow that moment had become very vivid, very real. He waited as the details came back to him, and the mirthful sounds filled the room as each man gave expression to the humor of the situation in his own way.

That the scene their minds had conjured up was perhaps funnier to them than it would have been to a layman was due to the fact that they knew the purpose of the ferrotyper so well and the importance of keeping its glossy surface clean at all times.

"Didn't he say anything?" Shelby asked when he could get his breath.

"Yeah," said Casey. "Exactly three words. I can see him now. Sitting there, very serious, a sort of preoccupied look on his face. He took his first bite and started chewing and then he took another bite. He held the sandwich out and scowled at it. He looked at me and then, before he took his next bite, he said: 'It needs salt.'"

Lanvin whooped. Shelby exploded and nearly fell off the chair. Casey stood up and straightened his hat. He was laughing too now, partly because of the picture in his mind and partly because of the infectious sounds of his colleagues.

"Then what?" Shelby said when he was able to catch his breath.

"Nothing," Casey said. "He ate the sandwich, put on his cap, and walked out."

"What did you do?"

"I thought I'd better leave, too, so I did."

"What about the ferrotyper? I mean, it was greasy, wasn't it?"

"Sure it was greasy," Casey said. "Cleary found that out a little later. He developed some film and made prints and slapped them on the ferrotyper. When they dried they were a mess. He didn't know why. He didn't find out until the next day, but right then there was only one thing he could do. He had to turn the heat off until the thing cooled and then work on that metal until it was clean again."

He went out then, the sound of their chuckling still in his ears, and as he rode down in the elevator he knew he felt a lot better. This, he told himself, was the way to think of Johnny Keeler. The good things, the fun times, the warm thoughts—these were the things to remember, this was the way Keeler would want it, and knowing this, Casey was able to sustain the mood all through dinner. It was not until he had been home for some time that the telephone rang and brought his thoughts back to the reality of the moment. The caller was

Julius Levy and what he had to say was as puzzling as it was surprising.

"Can you be at my office at ten o'clock in the morning?" the lawyer asked.

"Sure, I guess so," Casey said.

"I want to go over Johnny's will with his daughter and son-in-law and that time is convenient for them."

"But why me?" Casey said, not understanding.

"You're in the will."

"I'm what?"

"There's a paragraph that concerns you. I think you should be here. . . . Also, the funeral is Tuesday and you're one of the pallbearers."

4

JULIUS LEVY'S law offices were like the man himself, neat, tidy, and conservative. Moving in from the hall at five minutes of ten the next morning, Casey came first to a modestly furnished anteroom which was empty at the moment. A small window had been cut into the opposite wall and the middle-aged stenographer who had been with Levy for many years saw him at once and opened the door adjacent to the window.

The second room was not much larger than the first. The only other occupant, aside from the secretary, was an apple-cheeked youth named Goldmann who was a law-school graduate but had not yet been admitted to the bar. The secretary said Casey could go right in, and she preceded him across the room and opened the door beyond.

Levy's private office was a squarish corner room furnished with a good rug, a flattop desk, four or five leather-backed chairs, a steel filing cabinet with a simulated wood finish, and a lot of books. Levy rose from behind his desk and shook hands as the secretary closed the door. He said good morning and

Casey replied, but his eyes were already busy. Two things caught his attention. On the floor and stacked against one wall were two leather equipment bags and some additional cardboard boxes of various sizes, most of them small. These things, he understood at once, contained Johnny Keeler's cameras and equipment, and now, his glance moving to the desk, he saw the two metal boxes which contained the negatives Keeler had accumulated over the years.

"I don't get it, Julius," he said. "I mean being in the will."

"You will," Levy said. "He counted on you. He knew you'd understand. I can tell you very quickly what it amounts to, but I have to go through the formalities and I want his daughter to be present when I do. . . . These are yours," he said and touched the two film boxes. "This letter goes with them. You can read it when you get time. The rest of this"—he gestured toward the equipment on the floor—"is to be sold, but you're the executor, so to speak. You are to decide how it is to be sold, and when, and how much it's worth. You're an expert and it's up to you to get the best possible prices for the benefit of the estate."

Casey took the legal-size envelope, saw his name written on the front, and noticed it carried a wax seal. It was not bulky, and as he turned it over in his hands, the intercom on the desk buzzed. When Levy flipped the key Casey could hear the secretary say: "Mrs. Jensen is here."

Casey said: "Alma?"

The lawyer nodded and went over to the door to meet the woman. He shook hands formally and he gave her a grave good morning.

She said: "Good morning, Mr. Levy. . . . Good morning, Jack."

Casey said: "Good morning," and was again impressed by her face and figure, and the way she wore her clothes. It was cold out, a raw spring morning with the wind in sharply from the east, and his first thought—that she was dressed in black —was soon modified. As she moved past the window where the light was better and took the chair Levy arranged for her, he saw that she was wearing a tailored wool suit of dark gray, with an outer coat to match and a small smart-looking hat that looked as if it had been made of the same material.

As Levy stepped back behind his desk, he said it was good of her to come.

"I appreciate the fact that it may be a little awkward for you," he added, "but I want Johnny Keeler's daughter to understand his intentions. You won't have to stay," he said, as if to reassure her. "There is a bequest for you in the form of an insurance policy and once that has been covered it will be quite all right if you want to leave."

"I'm sure I would prefer it that way," she said.

Sheila Garrett neé Keeler arrived with her husband as Casey was lighting a cigarette. He came to his feet as Levy greeted the couple. He said he thought they had met Mrs. Jensen and Casey; they said they had, nodding politely but with no great warmth. While chairs were arranged for them, Casey had a chance to study them, to recall the small, dark-haired woman who had been Keeler's daughter.

She looked very smart in her simple black dress and mink jacket, and although she was still in her late twenties, her small-boned figure had taken on a plumpness that he did not remember. Her oval face, while rather pretty, had a somewhat haughty look and the dark eyes beneath the penciled brows held an aloof expression. By contrast, her husband was big and blond and impressively tailored. When called upon, he could affect a certain superficial charm, and any TV producer given to type casting, and needing a playboy character, would have picked him without hesitation.

Casey did not pay close attention to the legal phraseology in the first paragraph of Keeler's will, but it surprised him to learn that his was the first name mentioned. In substance, Keeler's wishes in the matter of his collection of negatives had already been explained, but when the cameras and equipment were mentioned there was one thought that had not been expressed. This was a matter of commission: twenty per cent of the total realized value of these possessions was to be paid to him for his trouble, the balance going to Alma Jensen.

Levy paused here to peer at Casey over his glasses. "I assume you will agree to act for the estate in this matter?"

"Certainly," Casey said, touched by the simple expression of Keeler's faith in him. "But he didn't have to stick in that twenty per cent part."

"He knew that," Levy said. "It was just something he wanted to do."

He glanced again at the will in his hands, and when Casey heard Alma Jensen's name mentioned, he picked out certain words: ". . . my dear friend and companion, for her devotion, loyalty, and affection during the past three years. . . ."

By that time Casey understood that the woman had been named beneficiary in a twenty-thousand-dollar insurance policy, and somehow the knowledge surprised him less than it did the woman. He heard her small gasp and saw her lips part. He also saw Sheila Garrett's mouth tighten, as though it was an effort on her part to keep from protesting. She looked sharply at her husband, who shrugged silently and glanced away; then Levy was supplying additional details not in the will.

"I will keep the policy temporarily, Mrs. Jensen," he said, "since there are certain forms to be taken care of. But the insurance representative will be in touch with you direct. He will explain the various options of payment. If you have any questions—"

He let the sentence dangle as he leaned back. He put his hands palm down on the desk as though preparing to rise. Seeing this, the woman stood up, her cheeks flushed and her eyes lowered.

She said: "Thank you, Mr. Levy." Then, as if to herself and in a voice that was no more than a whisper: "He didn't have to do that. He already—"

Levy heard, and he cut her off. "It was not done on impulse, I can assure you, Mrs. Jensen. He discussed the matter with me more than once and that was what he wanted."

Casey was already on his feet, and finally Stan Garrett stood up. He watched Levy move with Alma Jensen to the door and escort her out. Sheila Garrett said nothing as the door closed, but if anything, her red mouth was even tighter.

Levy resumed his reading, and this time Casey's thoughts centered on the couple and he realized again how little he knew about the woman. He recalled Keeler's displeasure when she informed him she was going to get married. He knew Keeler had gone so far as to threaten to cut her out of his will and for a moment he wondered if this could be true.

He knew she had ignored the threat. She had simply gone off with Garrett and got married. They had lived for a while in Garrett's apartment and later had found a larger place out beyond Cleveland Circle. He had heard that she worked part time as a doctor's receptionist, though he did not know whether this was for economic reasons or as an antidote to boredom.

But of one thing he was certain: she was seldom seen after hours with her husband, and considering Garrett's activities, this seemed somewhat surprising. Adding up the things he knew and the things he had heard about the man, Casey found himself sharing some of Keeler's objections to Garrett as a son-in-law. The fact that Keeler had never been close to his daughter did not mean he did not want the best for her, and in many respects Garrett's reputation left something to be desired.

His chief stock in trade seemed to be not a superior I.Q. but a personality based none too soundly on his blond good looks, a breezy self-confidence, and a smooth if superficial technique that seemed especially effective where women were concerned. Such attributes had made a salesman of sorts out of him; at one time or another he had tried cars, bonds, and real estate. More recently he had been doing promotion work for an organization called Flynn Enterprises, the guiding hand of which belonged to one John Flynn, who had made a lot of money in contracting and in the trucking business. Flynn was also a figure of considerable power in political circles, though he had never run for office, and in more recent years he had made additional investments in certain race tracks, the dog track south of the city, and the local professional football team.

It was at such sporting events and certain night spots that Stan Garrett was usually seen. Within the limits of Casey's experience, Garrett was seldom alone. Sometimes he was with a group of one kind or another; more often he would be seen with a woman companion. The fact that he did not go out with the same one for any length of time indicated that such associations were temporary, and this was further testimony to the theory that he fancied himself a ladies' man and was ready to prove it whenever the opportunity presented itself. Such liaisons, Casey knew, were no proof of unfaithfulness and if his wife objected to them there was no public record of it. . . .

A loud and disdainful grunt from Garrett jerked Casey's thoughts back to the moment as Levy, reading from the will, said:

" 'Because of my active dislike for Stanley Garrett and my disapproval of his manners, morals, and philosophy; because it is my belief that he would soon dissipate any substantial amount of money he could get his hands on—' "

"All right, all right." Garrett's words were blunt and irritable. "I know what Keeler thought of me. So does everyone else. Sheila's heard it for years." He glanced at his wife. "I mean, do we have to go through this again, darling?"

"No." Sheila looked at Levy. "I agree with my husband. I know all about my father's opinions. I know he disapproved of me, too, but I don't wish to be reminded of it now. Couldn't you just, please, tell us what is to happen to his estate?"

Levy eyed her with disapproval and cleared his throat. "I was about to say that your father directed that his estate be placed in trust."

"What kind of trust?" Garrett asked.

"A life trust for Mrs. Garrett. That is to say, she will receive the income as long as she lives. Upon her death it will be divided among her children, if any, when they come of age. If there are no children, provisions have been made to—" He stopped and let the room grow quiet. When he continued there was a note of gentle sarcasm in his voice. "But then you're not interested in your father-in-law's opinions. I'll give you a copy of the will when you go out and you can see for yourself."

"And what will the estate amount to, Mr. Levy?" Sheila Garrett asked. "I mean roughly."

Levy put down the will and leaned back in his chair again. "I'm glad to say your father did very well for a man who never drew a large salary. Over the years he made some excellent investments—"

"You mean you made them."

"I beg your pardon?"

"He respected you. If any good investments were made I think you probably made them."

"Be that as it may," Levy said, "he did quite well. At current market prices I'd say the stocks and bonds he owned would amount to better than a hundred thousand dollars. In addition, he had a hundred-and-twenty-thousand-dollar equity in an apartment building—"

"The one Alma Jensen lives in, no doubt."

Levy ignored that one. In the same unruffled tone he said: "There's also a second insurance policy for thirty thousand dollars that should take care of most of the taxes and administrative expenses."

"Are you the administrator?" Garrett said.

"I am."

"And the executor?"

"Co-executor. With the Third National Bank."

"So how much income will Sheila get?"

"With reasonable safety I'd say not more than four per cent. Say a minimum of nine thousand, possibly more as time goes on."

"Fair enough." Garrett stood up, his good-looking face

bland and apparently unconcerned. "I guess that covers it, doesn't it?"

"Except for some details that probably wouldn't interest you," Levy said.

Sheila Garrett rose and adjusted her fur jacket. Her face was relaxed now and there were no signs of pique or irritation to mar its prettiness. She walked straight up to Levy and offered her hand.

"Thank you, Mr. Levy," she said. "I know you don't really approve of me any more than my father did, but I want you to know I appreciate what you did for him. You were one of his best friends and I hope eventually you'll be one of mine. I'm awfully glad you'll be handling the trust."

Levy looked a little flustered at her forthrightness, and as the couple started out and Casey came to his feet, he spoke.

"Will you wait, Jack? There are some things I would like to discuss with you."

Casey said yes, but his mind was already on a job he had to do and now he asked if he could use the telephone. Levy said yes. He said the one on the right was the outside line.

The number Casey dialed was familiar to him and belonged to the owner of a hole-in-the-wall camera shop on Stuart Street. His name was Ralph Tyler and he was both a connoisseur and an expert mechanic where cameras were concerned. The picture-taking public at large had never heard of him and would not have been admitted to his shop if they had. For he dealt only with people he liked and this limited his clientele to most professionals and a few select amateurs who had the proper respect for their equipment. In addition to repairing cameras, he bought, sold, and traded them and Casey knew he was the only man in town who could properly dispose of Keeler's equipment.

He explained what he had in mind when he had identified himself, and Tyler listened until he finished.

"Sure," he said. "Sure I'll handle the stuff. But I have to tell you now that one of those cameras in Johnny's collection is probably mine."

"How do you mean?"

"He borrowed it a couple of days ago. Said he wanted to try it out."

For another second or so Casey groped for an answer, and it finally came to him as he recalled the new camera he had seen on Keeler's bench Saturday night.

"That rapid-sequence job with the new flash unit?"

"That's the one."

"Oh—I wondered about that. I didn't think I'd ever seen it before."

"I've only had it in the shop a few weeks."

"Okay. I'll tell Julius Levy about it. Suppose I bring the stuff down after lunch."

"It's almost lunch time now," Tyler said. "Bring it when you're ready, and stop and pick up a couple of sandwiches —ham-and-cheese on rye for me—and I'll supply the coffee."

When Levy came in and closed the door Casey told him about Ralph Tyler. He explained that only through Tyler could they get the best prices. He said that in his opinion the estate would get more money in the long run if Tyler could sell the equipment a piece at a time as opportunity offered rather than accept a lump sum, which would necessarily be smaller. He also spoke of the camera Keeler had borrowed and Levy nodded.

"I'm glad you told me," he said. "Now's the time to know about such things. What I want you to do is make a list of everything, on the typewriter, please, with a carbon. I'll have to have it for the tax people because they try to capitalize on everything and this way I'll have an accurate record made by an expert."

He sat down behind the desk, his eyes thoughtful behind the glasses. He glanced at the two metal boxes containing Keeler's old negatives and finally tapped the top one lightly with the tips of his fingers.

"But what I really wanted to talk to you about are these. You haven't read the letter yet, have you? Well, why don't you do it now? It may influence you in some way in what I have to say. Sit over there by the window. I've got a few things to straighten up here on my desk, so take your time."

5

WHEN CASEY had settled himself in the chair and got a cigarette going, he opened the envelope and saw that it contained a single sheet of bond paper. The letter was typewritten, but when he saw the salutation he stopped reading and his glance slipped away.

Dear Flash is what it said, and this was a nickname used only by those who had known him a long time ago. It originated in the fact that when he had come to work as a kid flashbulbs had not reached their present state of perfection. There were times then when a flash-pan or spread-light were necessary and the agent of illumination was magnesium powder. Because of its volatility, care was needed in its handling and the resulting flash was spectacular to behold but not without an element of danger for the careless.

There had been one occasion when, in his inexperience, he had used too much powder and nearly set a room on fire, and someone had tagged him with that name and it had stuck. In these days most people simply called him Casey. Some, especially women, preferred Jack; still others, mostly the young who had been taught the proper uses of respect, called him Mr. Casey. He responded to all of them without resentment and now, bringing his eyes back to the letter, he remembered these things and the lines of his mouth softened.

You're the only guy I know, it read, *that maybe can understand why I haven't destroyed these things a long time ago. I guess all photographers have a collection of negatives they like for one reason or another. To another photographer they're nothing. To you they're something*

*special and once you start to hold a few out maybe you
get cracked on the subject—I guess I did—and the longer
you keep them the harder they are to destroy. I couldn't
make myself throw them away but you can; that's why
I'm dropping the problem in your lap.*

*The plates you'll find are old. I think they might be of
some interest to a student or a researcher and maybe you
should ask the University or the Public Library if they
want them. The rest of them have no monetary value except to a blackmailer. Some could be dangerous to some
people. If I hadn't decided that you could handle the job
for me I would have had to get rid of them myself but
personally I like it better this way.*

*I have an idea that, aside from the plates, they should
be burned. I never gave away a negative in my life and
I'm at least consistent because when you read this I won't
be here. Maybe you'll want to go through them and see if
there's anything you want. I doubt if I would in your
shoes because it's too much of a job and the picture you
didn't take yourself never means anything much because
you can go out and buy a similar one that is probably
just as good or better.*

*Take care of it for me, will you, Flash? If you want to
give any of them away I can trust your judgement because I know you'd never let even one of them get into
the wrong hands. I guess my suggestion would be to take
a look if you want, keep what you want, then burn the
rest. But the decision is yours, and having written this,
I'll no longer have it on my mind even if I live to be a
hundred.*

With admiration and respect as always,
Johnny

Casey lowered the letter and stared out the window at the
building across the street, an odd thickness in his throat and
confusion in his mind. A certain sadness mingled with his concern, and because he needed a little more time, he was very

deliberate as he folded the letter and reinserted it in the envelope. When he was ready he looked at Levy.

"Okay, Julius," he said. "What's the rest of it?"

"There isn't any rest, actually. These films are yours now and I assume, now that you have read the letter, that you know how Johnny felt about them."

"You said you wanted to talk about something," Casey said. "Yes."

Levy hesitated, stroking his forehead with two fingers of his left hand. Whether from embarrassment or indecision, he seemed to be groping for words and this in itself was unusual.

"I find this rather difficult to phrase," he said finally, "but a certain party has been in touch with me. He's worried about one or two of those films. To put it more directly, he wants them." Levy gestured emptily. "I explained the situation. I told him the films were no longer mine and that what happened to them was up to you."

"You didn't open the box?" Casey asked and then, realizing what he had implied and seeing the look on the lawyer's face, he was suddenly embarrassed and went on quickly. "I'm sorry. I didn't mean that the way it sounded."

"I know you didn't. I was physically able to pull out those drawers and examine the films, but morally and ethically it was impossible. When I took them from Johnny's safe I taped them"—he pointed to the two bands of cellophane tape that securely sealed the metal boxes—"and here they are."

"Who's the guy?"

"I'm afraid I can't tell you that. But an offer of five thousand dollars has been made for the proper films."

Casey repeated the figure and whistled softly. Wrinkles deepened in his brows and his dark gaze was speculative. He thought again of the letter and Keeler's words of caution. He remembered, too, some of Keeler's parties and his compulsion to photograph anything and everything at any time. When he could find no answer he could accept, he stood up.

"You don't know why this person wants them?"

"No."

"Or what he intends to do with them?"

"No. Neither have I any recommendation to make one way or the other. I merely agreed to present the offer."

Casey lifted one hand aimlessly and let it fall. "I don't know what to say, Julius. I'm not interested in the five thousand as such."

"I know you're not."

"Offhand I'd say the answer is no, but I'm not going to say it now. I've got to think it over. . . . I'd like to get this other stuff down to Ralph Tyler's right away," he added. "Can I leave the boxes here for a while?"

"Certainly." Levy rose and moved over to the filing cabinet that was made of steel and looked like wood. He opened the bottom drawer, which was empty. He put the two boxes inside and closed the drawer. He pointed to the lock at the top which secured all drawers when the key was turned.

"They'll be safe here," he said. "I'll pass the word that you're thinking this other matter over. Young Goldmann"—he nodded towards the outer office—"will give you a hand with that equipment. Let me know what you and Tyler decide and don't forget my list."

Ralph Tyler's camera shop was just wide enough for some show cases, the row of shelves behind them, and a passageway from the entrance to his living quarters beyond the curtain at the rear. There was no name on the door, only a number, and his two-by-four display window was usually empty.

Casey, arriving shortly before one with the youth from Levy's office, carried Keeler's equipment into the back room. When Goldmann had left, Tyler locked the door and Casey brought out the sandwiches he had picked up on the way down. When he had unfolded the wax paper, he shucked off his balmacaan and placed his hat on top of it. While he was doing this, Tyler brought two cups from the adjacent cubbyhole which served as his kitchen, a thin, long-faced man with thick-lensed glasses and an untidy look. His sweater was out at the elbows and he wore no tie, and now he moved to the

electric hot plate that stood on the table at the kitchen end
of the room. There was always hot coffee waiting here and to
those he liked it was his custom to offer a cup regardless of
the time of day; those special friends who really rated received an additional soupçon of good brandy to flavor the
coffee.

When he had served Casey, he moved the equipment cases
close to a lumpy-looking studio couch and unzipped them.
He began to take out cameras and lense cases and when he
came to the new rapid-sequence model Keeler had borrowed
he set it aside. Turning to examine the spindle on his cluttered
workbench, he removed a paper and offered it to Casey, who,
with a sandwich in one hand and the cup in the other, merely
scowled at it.

"What's that?"

"A receipt. Johnny signed it when he took the camera."

"How come?"

"How come what? I lend lots of things. I like to keep a
record of who's got them."

"Oh. I was wondering if you figured something might happen to him."

"Something did happen to him, didn't it?"

Casey grunted. He told Tyler that he had seen the camera
Saturday night. He said he hadn't seen a flash unit like that
before and he wondered where Keeler got it.

"When did he borrow it?"

"Friday."

"Did he just happen to come in?"

"Sure." Tyler said. "He didn't come in to buy it; he didn't
know I had it until I showed it to him. You know how he was.
Anything new, he wanted to try it out. I said sure, and he said
he'd bring it back the first of the week. What's so unusual
about that?"

"Nothing."

"Oh. I thought something was bugging you." Tyler sat
down and a couch spring protested under his weight. He ate
his sandwich absently and his other hand was busy sorting

out lenses and filters. "How do you want to handle this?" he asked finally. "Do you want me to give you an estimate on the works and make an offer?"

Casey said no. He said he had an idea the items would bring better prices if Tyler could sell a piece at a time when the right person came along.

"In other words," Tyler said, "I take the stuff on consignment and sell it where and when I can?"

Casey said yes and explained the clause that Keeler had used in his will.

"All I want is the best price," he said. "You take the twenty per cent."

"I'll take ten and you take the other ten," Tyler said. "If I have to do any work on any of the cameras—and I don't think I will because Johnny kept his stuff in good condition— I'll charge for my time and take it off the selling price."

"Fair enough," Casey said. "Where's your typewriter? Let's get started on the list."

It took them the best part of an hour to complete the job of cataloguing the equipment. A place had been cleared at the cluttered desk for Tyler's battered typewriter and Casey picked out a description of each item with his two-fingered technique. He made it as accurate as possible, adding the manufacturer's number when one was given. Tyler, using a jeweler's loup from time to time, opened each camera and checked the mechanism for scratches and signs of wear. A tentative price was added for each piece and they agreed that such prices were the minimums for the tax people and that Tyler would make every effort to get a better selling price.

When they finished Casey had a top copy and two carbons. He gave the second one to Tyler and pocketed the other two so he would have one for himself and one for Levy. He refused a second cup of coffee and was putting on his hat and coat when Tyler said:

"What's going to happen to all those films that Keeler saved?"

Casey tapped his chest with his thumb and Tyler's eyes opened behind the thick lenses.

"You've got them?"

"He left them to me."

"Couldn't bring himself to destroy them, hunh?" Tyler shook his head. "I bet he's got some choice items there."

"I don't know," Casey said. "I haven't looked at them."

"Are you going to?"

"I don't know."

"Well, what are you going to do with them?"

"I don't know that either," Casey said, and as he started through the shop on his way to the door, he knew that this was indeed the truth.

6

FOR THE REST of the afternoon Casey gave his time to the *Express*. He was on his way back from Ralph Tyler's shop when the police radio tipped him off to an accident on the Riverway and he made the scene about thirty seconds after the fire department. A rear-end collision had set one car afire, and while there were no serious injuries, the blaze was briefly spectacular and he got a couple of shots that pleased him. Later he had to do a job for the business office, and to keep this particular advertiser happy he made several prints. As a result, it was nearly seven o'clock before he decided to call it a day.

When it came to thinking about dinner, he created a mental menu and by process of elimination found he had a hankering for oysters. This took him downtown to the Old Oyster House, where he sat at the bar and watched the counterman open a dozen Cotuits for him. He ate these slowly and with relish as his stew was being prepared, and by the time he finished his coffee he decided that one additional item would make his meal complete. A brandy was what he wanted, but since the Oyster House served only wine and beer, he drove to a place located about three blocks from his apartment.

It was called the Melody Club, a name apparently derived from the piano at the rear, which was presided over by a colored man playing softly and with restraint. There were about six customers at the bar when Casey handed over his hat and coat to the smiling hat-check girl at the entrance. Because the room was narrow, there was only one long row of tables between the bar and the semicircular booths, about half of which were occupied at the moment. It was not the sort of place that attracted those who wanted to whoop it up. There was no other entertainment, the lighting was subdued, and if the piano player was not a top performer, he played easily and made the most of a good left hand and a full-chorded right that kept his arpeggios simple, crisp, infrequent.

He was playing *Memories Of You* and doing very well with it in his unaffected way as Casey slid onto a bar stool. "Good evening, Albert," he said and nodded toward the piano as the barman approached. "He's always the same, isn't he?"

"Good evening, Mr. Casey," Albert said. "Yes, he is. The customers seem to like him that way. Bourbon?"

"Brandy tonight, Albert. Martels will be all right, with a little soda on the side."

Albert put a small snifter glass on the bar, filled it half full of brandy, dropped two ice cubes into a small highball glass, and added soda. Casey got a cigarette going before he tasted the brandy and took time to look the room over. Most of the customers were strangers to him, but a man sitting in a booth with a pretty brunette gave him a small salute and Casey returned the gesture without knowing who he was. He was half-finished with his drink and feeling very content when the woman came in.

He saw her from the corner of his eye as she stopped in the doorway. He saw her start in his direction, but he did not glance around. When she kept coming he assumed that she was going to take the bar stool next to him, and because he knew much about the technique of some single women in bars, this did not surprise him either. But this time he was wrong. She did not take the stool but stopped beside him and put her hand on his arm.

"Hello, Jack," she said.

He turned then, recognizing her. "Hi," he said.

She was about average height and of medium build. She wore a dark red dress, topped by a black cloth coat. She was bareheaded and her blondness was of the chemical kind, though not extreme. He thought she was about twenty-seven or twenty-eight and the subdued lighting was kind to her. Her makeup was not as noticeable here and the weary worldliness he had sometimes seen in her face was less apparent. Her name was Fay Novak and she began instantly to talk, an odd breathlessness in her voice and manner and a bright look in her blue eyes that he was unable to diagnose.

He understood that she was asking him how he was, and where he had been, and why didn't she ever see him any more. Such talk in itself was unusual because he did not know her that well. Still not understanding what had motivated this new interest in him, he answered none of her questions but asked one of his own.

"How about a drink?"

She did not hesitate, but her agitation was somewhat less obvious, and when she nodded she found a small smile for him.

"All right."

"What would you like?"

"What are you drinking?"

He told her and she said she would have the same thing. Casey spoke to the barman and nothing more was said until she was served. Then, looking at her glass, she said:

"Could we sit down for a minute, please? I'd like to talk to you."

Casey said why not and led the way to an empty booth near the front, waiting until she slid along the leather-covered banquette before he sat down opposite her. The breathlessness, the look of agitation, had left her by then, but although her voice became quickly casual and a little too indifferent, the worried expression remained in the shadowed blue eyes.

"How many beds do you have at your place?"

"One."

"Oh."

"Oh what?"

She tipped one hand. "I thought if you had two I might rent one for the night. I don't suppose you could sleep on the couch."

"The couch is too small for me," Casey said. "Who are you running from?"

"What gave you that idea?"

"You looked a little out of breath when you came in. You were just a little jumpy, weren't you?"

"Who does a girl generally run from?"

"A guy?"

"Who else?"

"Are you still working in the lounge at the Parkview?"

She nodded.

"Some customer bugging you?"

She nodded again and Casey took a sip of brandy and paused a moment to refresh his memory about Fay Novak. The mental dossier he fashioned was sketchy because he had never been very close to her. He had seen her here and there during the past few years and they always said hello and maybe took a minute or two to talk about this or that. During that time he had bought her an occasional drink and twice, when he had been helping close up the place where she was working, he had driven her home, but not recently.

She had been married when he first met her, but she had been divorced for three or four years now and supported herself by a variety of jobs, all in the same general category. She had worked as a hat-check girl in two or three clubs here and on the Cape; she had been a waitress, a barmaid, a hostess. The last time he had seen her she was working in the lounge of the Parkview Hotel, which, if not strictly first class, was an old and respectable hotel.

"Aren't you off early tonight?" he asked finally.

"Yes. Because of this character. I didn't want to make a scene, so I left."

"Why don't you sleep in your own place?"

"Because, as if I didn't know better, I gave him my address when he was in last night," she said. "He's from out of town and he'll be leaving in the morning, but he's got a load on tonight and I don't trust him."

Casey waited, unable to see her expression because her face was angled away from him as she toyed with her glass. He was wondering, too, because although the explanation seemed simple enough, there was an intangible something about the words that left him unconvinced.

"Okay," he said. "I'll drive you home. I'll take you right up to your apartment and you can lock yourself in."

"And maybe an hour from now he'll come banging on the door."

"Then call the cops."

"That would be just dandy. They'd wake up the whole house and everybody'd think it was my fault and tomorrow the landlord would probably throw me out. Not tonight," she said and shook her head. She finished her brandy, frowned at the glass; then her expression changed. "Wait a minute. I've got an idea."

She had a large, patent-leather handbag on her lap. She started to fumble with the clasp; then stopped and glanced up. "Have you got a dime?"

Casey found one and she slid out of the seat and started for the telephone booth in the foyer. She put the handbag on the seat, but because she was hurrying she was careless. The surface of the handbag was slippery and so was the seat. It was also slightly rounded and Casey saw the bag start to slip. He reached under the table in an effort to grab it, missed, and the bag thudded heavily to the floor.

Still crouched and reaching under the table, he got hold of

the bag and drew it towards him. He straightened on the seat, the bag in his lap; then, in the act of replacing it, he stopped. He was not sure why. The bag had made a funny sound when it hit the floor, and as he balanced it on his hand, it seemed strangely heavy. He squeezed the sides experimentally, not looking for anything special but wondering. He could tell that there was something hard inside and now, his curiosity prodding him, he unfastened the catch.

What he saw told him why the bag seemed heavy. He was still holding it under the table but he could see the gun, and when he took it out he discovered that it was a short-barreled revolver with wooden stocks. A glance at the muzzle told him it was a .22, and as he flipped the cylinder out, he saw that it held seven or eight rim-fire cartridges. He also saw that one of them bore the imprint of the hammer.

All this took no more than a few seconds and he hesitated no longer but replaced the gun, closed the bag, and put it over on the seat. He leaned back, finished his brandy, and took a sip of soda. He considered again the story Fay had told him, but he tried not to think about the gun.

It was none of his business. He was sorry he found it, and that's what he got for being so nosy. The fact that the gun was there was further indication that the girl had indeed been scared of something. Beyond that he refused to speculate, and he was relieved to see her moving back to the booth.

She was smiling now. Nice teeth made the smile attractive and helped erase the strain and weariness he had seen in her face.

"It's okay, honey," she said, sounding relieved. "I've got me a bed with a friend. . . . A girl friend," she added when she saw the doubt in his glance. "If you'll just get me a cab, I'll be out of your hair."

She made no attempt to sit down as Casey rose. "I'll drive you wherever you want to go," he said.

"No." She shook her head. "I'd rather have a taxi."

Casey shrugged and said okay. He followed her out into the foyer and reclaimed his hat and coat. When they got outside there was no cab waiting and he turned her toward the nearest intersection. They did not have to wait long before a cruising taxi spotted them and swooped to a stop at the curb. When Casey opened the door the driver greeted him with an easy familiarity that many people used.

"Hi, Casey."

Casey looked at him, finding the thick-browed, blue-jowled face vaguely familiar but unable to put a name to it.

"Hi," he said. "Is it Tony?"

"Rudy. Rudy Kowalchik."

"Sure. The lady will tell you where she wants to go," he added. "Drive carefully, Rudy, and take her right up to her door, will you?"

Casey watched the cab pull away and then walked back to his own car and climbed in. As he angled out from the curb, the tubes in the police radio warmed and he began to hear the voice of the dispatcher at headquarters. The sound was so familiar that he had learned to listen with only half an ear; he could be completely absorbed in his own thoughts and still be conscious of any words or phrases that were the least bit unusual.

Now he could hear calls being made to cruising cars, the responses that came, the time announcements that were given at regular intervals. Car so-and-so was called, answered, and was told to proceed to such-and-such a corner and investigate a disturbance. Car so-and-so was directed to a factory in the south end and told to contact the night watchman. The third call commanded Casey's immediate attention because he had not heard it before.

Certain signals had a special meaning for those who could translate them. A shooting, for instance, or a homicide or a suspicion of homicide, might be designated by a certain letter or series of letters. When such a signal was heard by the various reporters and photographers who were cruising about in company cars, they would all converge on the scene, thereby creating a certain amount of confusion and lost motion. The frequent changing of signals was a self-protective device on the part of the officials to thwart such unwanted interference. There was nothing they could do to prevent police reporters at headquarters from following up a crime, but they tried, when they could, to delay other newsmen listening in on radio signals.

What Casey heard now was the dispatcher talking to car twenty-one. When he got his reply he mentioned an address and said: "Signal KY. KY."

Casey had no idea what KY meant. It could have been nothing more than someone who was drunk and disorderly and needed picking up, but the address given was not far, and since he had nothing else to do, his response was characteristic.

He was in the middle of the block on a one-way street and he immediately stepped on the gas and began to angle toward the left side of the street so he could make the turn at the corner. In the process, he cut off a startled citizen, who gave him an angry blast of the horn, and then he was turning into the side street and already planning his route.

The address was not far from Atlantic Avenue, a block of old three- and four-storied brick buildings, most of which had stores and shops on the ground floor and offices above. The narrow, one-way street was a scene of daytime activity, but it was quiet and dark now except for the dim night lights that burned behind a few shop windows. As Casey whipped the sedan around the corner and straightened out, he saw that although his was not the first car to arrive, it was close.

A police sedan was already parked halfway down the block, and he saw the two uniformed officers hurry across the sidewalk and disappear into a doorway to the left. There was plenty of room to park at this hour, and he stopped a car's length behind the police cruiser. Then, reaching into the back of the car, he grabbed his camera, and slid out from behind the wheel.

The doorway he headed for stood between a plumbing-supply shop with darkened windows and a radio store with a lighted front. The outer door stood open, and he went through the narrow entryway, seeing the directory fastened to one wall but not looking at it. There was no elevator, and the stairs mounted directly ahead of him. A single corridor on the second floor led from front to back, and when he saw the light spilling out from an open door near the rear, he headed for it.

It was not until he glanced at the name which had been lettered on the frosted glass panel of the door that he knew where he was. As he stepped into the tiny outer office, the faint sense of excitement which had up until now been dormant expanded swiftly and took hold of him. For he knew now that Clem Alpert was the tenant here and he was ready to accept the fact that this was no routine call.

The light was brighter in the second office, and the two officers quickly inspected him with narrow-eyed surprise. The one who stood near the end of the desk was tall and husky and no more than twenty-five or -six. The one who knelt just beyond was older, and it was perhaps fortunate that he knew Casey.

"Hello, Casey," he said. "How the hell did you get here so soon?"

"I heard the dispatcher's signal."

"What signal?" the young one said with some suspicion.

"KY," Casey said and went into immediate action before they had a chance to consider the matter too thoroughly and come up with some objection.

Without paying attention to details, he already had the impression that the office had been ransacked. The slender form of Clem Alpert, oddly crumpled now, lay between the desk and the wall, and the swivel chair had been upset beside it. The center drawer was upside down across the thighs, as though it had been pulled out as Alpert fell backwards. The torso had come to rest with the head touching an overturned wastebasket. The sharp-featured face was visible only in profile, but Casey had seen and photographed a lot of dead men in his time, most of them victims of violence of one kind or another, and there was a look about them that he had come to recognize, an unmistakable something that defied descrip-

tion and was based on experience and instinct rather than
medical knowledge.

Clem Alpert had that look now as the light from the flash
unit burst upon his still figure. There was no sign of a wound,
no blood, but the impression remained as Casey took that first
picture standing alongside the older officer, who was still on
one knee.

He wound film as he backed away. He reached for a
straight-backed chair and swung it around in front of the desk.
When he stepped up on it to get a shot that angled down, the
young officer voiced a protest.

"Hey," he said. "Maybe you ought to wait until—"

"I've already finished," Casey said and pressed the shutter
release. "Clem Alpert, hunh?" he said as the light exploded.
"Dead?"

"Very." The older man stood up and blew his breath out.
"One in the chest almost dead center. . . . Where you going?"
he added sharply as Casey wheeled and started for the door.

"Got to get this to the car," Casey said, "and call the office.
I'll be back." Then, deciding that a small lie would do no harm,
he said: "I'm supposed to meet Lieutenant Logan here."

He was gone before they could think of an answer, and as
soon as he got back to his car, he flipped a switch on the
company radio and reached for the microphone.

"Car 61 calling the desk," he said. "Car 61." He repeated
this and waited until, a few seconds later, the radio squeaked
and a voice said: "Come in, Casey, what have you got?"

Casey told the city editor and it did not take long. The
death of a man like Alpert would not rate too much space. The
pictures he had would help the story, but that was no longer
a problem to him. He did not decide when a picture was used.
He only took them. He said he'd leave the film on the front
seat and to send an office boy over for it and now, aware that
other cars were pulling up behind him, he said he'd leave the
radio on so that the headquarters man could use it when he
got here.

7

CASEY WAS sitting alone in the outer office when Lieutenant Logan came in with Sergeant Manahan at his heels. Others had preceded Logan—two precinct detectives and a photographer and fingerprint man from headquarters—but Logan was a homicide man and the senior officer present.

He stopped when he spotted Casey, and his dark gaze narrowed. In that first second he looked more suspicious than surprised, and there was a faint but definite undertone of exasperation in his voice when he spoke.

"How long have you been here?"

"Quite a while."

"How'd you know about this?"

Casey hesitated, deciding he wouldn't overwork the bit about the KY signal.

"I saw the prowl car," he said, as if such a coincidence was the most natural thing in the world. "It was rolling pretty fast so I thought I'd tag along."

"I suppose you've already got your picture."

"Yep."

Logan glanced into the adjacent room, where the investigation was already in progress. He looked back at Casey and tightened his lips.

"You know I don't play favorites."

"I think I've heard you mention it."

"So either I let the other boys in or you go out and join them."

Casey sighed elaborately, expecting no other treatment. "I guess I'm invited out."

"You know you are."

"Okay. I'll wait."

"Don't bother."

"I've got time."

When he stepped into the hall, the newsmen who were being held at bay by a uniformed officer wanted to know how he got inside and he gave them the same story he had told Logan. They, too, accepted it because they had long maintained that Casey had more than his share of luck. In more rational moments they were also ready to admit that, like all top men in the field, much of Casey's luck was his own doing. He perhaps had more sources of information than they had, but he seemed also to have a knack of making his own breaks.

Now they asked what he knew and he told them. When he could he took Bronson, who was the police reporter for the *Express* on that shift, aside and asked if he'd seen Casey's car and used the radio. Bronson said yes. He said when he got some word from Logan he would phone in his follow-up.

There was considerable traffic in and out of the office as the investigation gained momentum. The deputy medical examiner came and was joined for a while by the captain of the precinct. Two ambulance attendants brought a stretcher and departed after some delay with a blanket-covered body, an event which was recorded on film by Aaron of the *News* and Leslie of the *Standard*.

The doctor came out and hurried off without comment, and finally Logan appeared with the captain to make a brief and none too explicit statement which made it official that: Clem Alpert had been shot once, and fatally, by a person or persons unknown; there were signs of a struggle; it was possible that Alpert had walked in and found a burglar who was searching the office and had made the mistake of resisting. Pending further investigation and laboratory reports, there was nothing more to add at that time.

The captain left when the announcement was over. Bronson gestured to Casey and went along with the captain. After a moment of indecision, the others followed since they had editions to make and no hope of learning anything more they could use here.

Casey alone remained. In no hurry now, he leaned against

the wall and lit a cigarette. When the police photographer came out, lugging his camera and equipment, he said goodnight. A precinct detective and a plain-clothes man departed shortly afterward, and the way Casey figured it, that left only Logan, Manahan, and one other detective.

When Manahan and the detective came out a little later, the sergeant spoke to the uniformed man on the door. As he saluted and started for the stairs, Casey pushed away from the wall. He dropped his cigarette and stepped on it.

"It ought to be about my turn," he said.

"I'll ask him," Manahan said and stepped back inside the office. He did not stay long. When he reappeared, he nodded and said: "Okay."

Logan's hat and coat were in the outer office. Moving into the next room, Casey found the lieutenant slumped in a chair that faced the desk. He gave no sign that he was aware of the photographer and this gave Casey a chance to inspect the room. The center drawer of the desk, which had been on the floor by Alpert's body, had now been placed on top; other drawers were open and looked as if they had been searched. Much of this, Casey knew, could have been done by Logan's men, but there was no question about the filing cabinet. The drawers had been forced, and now, as he moved past to an open door in the corner, he saw that what once might have been a closet had at some time been converted into a small darkroom, complete with enlarger, sink, and a stack of trays.

Casey had not expected this. But recalling the nature of Alpert's work, he realized that a camera and some developing equipment might be a necessary part of such activity. There were no negatives in sight, and because he wondered about this, he came back and placed himself in front of Logan.

"Did he have any films?"

"Plenty," Logan said, still not looking at him. "They were all over the floor. Kelsey," he said, referring to the police photographer, "took them with him, but I doubt if they'll help much on this. If the guy that went over this room wanted any special film, he probably got it."

"If it was here."

"Hunh?"

"If he searched only part of the place, you might figure he found what he wanted. If he went over everything, and it looks like he did, maybe he didn't get it because it wasn't here."

"He could have got scared off," Logan said, "or run out of time. There's a watchman that takes care of three of these buildings in the block. He comes around about once an hour just to check doors. He's the one that saw the light on here and put in the call."

He hoisted himself out of the chair and reached for a cigarette. He was about Casey's age and an inch or so shorter, which put him around six feet. His hair was dark like Casey's but straight and showed no gray, he had a much leaner look, and he was usually better dressed, not because his suits cost more but because he was more clothes-conscious and took better care of what he had. Now, giving Casey a thoughtful look, he said:

"What's your interest in this?"

"How do you mean?"

"You've spent a lot of time here tonight. It seems to me you're awfully damn curious about a guy who was never more than a two-bit operator. So why? Was he a buddy of yours, or do you know something I don't?"

Casey eased down in the chair that Logan had just vacated and took a moment to wonder what he could say. In the back of his mind there was the thought of Alpert and Johnny Keeler and two boxes of films that had been willed to him. He remembered the keys that were in the safe on Saturday night. Even then he had wondered just how long Alpert had been alone in that suite after Keeler had had his stroke.

It would be a simple matter for anyone so inclined to take the keys from the unconscious man's pocket, unlock the darkroom safe, and take out any negatives that might be important. He recalled the letter Keeler had left him and its words of caution. He considered again the odd offer that had come to Julius Levy. Already someone was ready to pay five thousand dollars for certain of those negatives. What a man like Alpert might do with them could, at the moment, only be a matter for conjecture.

It seemed now that Alpert *had* taken something from Keeler's safe, and in an effort to cash in on what he found, he might well have gone too far. But even as the thought came to him, Casey realized that he could not now confide in Logan. If he thought those films might supply a motive for murder, Logan would want them, all of them. He could get an order from the District Attorney which would enable him to seize them, and although Casey had great faith in the lieutenant's integrity, he was aware that there would be others who might have access to these negatives. Because this was a chance he did not want to take just yet, he shrugged and said:

"All I know is that Alpert was with Johnny Keeler when he had his stroke on Saturday night. According to Alpert, they were out together, but he wouldn't say why. I thought maybe you might have run into something here that would tie it up."

"Well, we haven't. Alpert was a wrong one as a cop. A little blackmail, if he thought there wasn't too much risk, would be right up his alley." He gestured with his cigarette. "So we've got a list of some of the people he worked for. We're going to have to check them all out. Manahan's out looking for his wife now. Maybe she can help—"

"His wife?"

"Sure. That blonde. I can't even remember her name. They got divorced three or four years ago, but she's been around town. . . ."

Casey did not hear the rest of it because what Logan had said jarred his mental processes and brought into sharp focus something he had completely forgotten. He sought no explanation as to why there should be this blind spot in his mind; he only knew it was so. Even when he had seen Alpert lying dead behind his desk, the thought had not occurred to him; the fact that Alpert had once been married never entered his head. Not much more than an hour ago he had been talking to Fay Novak. He knew that she had been married, too. Yet it had taken Logan to pinpoint the connection and remind him again that Fay Novak had once been Mrs. Clem Alpert.

Now, remembering the story she had told him, he still did not know what he should do about it. At the time he had accepted her explanation of the too-ardent customer who was giving her trouble. He was convinced that she had really been disturbed by something when she hurried into the Melody Club, but it was the gun he had found in her purse that bothered him most.

He did not want to get Fay Novak into trouble unnecessarily. He did not like to get anybody into trouble. But if it turned out that Alpert had been killed by a slug from a .22 caliber gun, that was something else again because he and Logan had been friends for a long time, a relationship which never could have existed if Casey was the sort who held out important information and tried to outsmart the police.

They had worked together often in the past, and he knew that although Logan tried to play by the book and did his best to be fair about giving information to the press, the personal element did enter into it. When he could, he was sometimes more confidential with Casey than he was with the average reporter or photographer. Yet even as he accepted this, Casey knew he could not tell Logan about Johnny Keeler's films. Because he was the guardian of those films now and Keeler trusted him to see that no one was hurt by the older man's odd complex about never giving a negative away.

It took no more than a second or two for all these things to pass through his mind, and now, feeling his way along, he said: "What kind of a gun killed him?"

"What difference does it make?"

Casey bristled at Logan's tone. He did not mean to nor was he aware of his reaction. It may have been some small feeling of guilt that put the edge in his voice, but he answered sharply.

"No difference," he said. "It's a logical question, isn't it?"

"It could be."

"Look." Casey took a breath and continued with exaggerated patience. "My camera's locked in the back of my car. I'm not looking for an exclusive story so I can run downstairs and call the city desk. I promise not to quote you if you're worried about it. One of the cops from the prowl car told me Alpert was shot once in the chest. I just wondered if he got hit with a .32 or a .45 or maybe a shotgun, but if it's some secret, forget I asked."

Casey's attack had a curious effect on Logan. It served to bring him out of the somewhat truculent mood, which had been intensified by the fact that he had no concrete leads. A small smile touched his mouth and was reflected in his dark eyes, and as he looked down at the burly brooding figure in the chair, he remembered other times when they had argued about a case.

In spite of the fact of their conflict of interest, Casey had long been one of his close friends. His own job was the apprehension of criminals, especially killers; Casey's interest was more simple. He wanted pictures, exclusive ones if possible, and because he knew most of the tricks of the trade, he was not above bargaining a bit when necessary. Unless a picture was involved, he was inclined to leave police work to those who were trained for the job, but Logan remembered times when Casey's outside contacts, personal knowledge, or just plain luck had helped solve a case that was giving the department difficulty.

Few things intimidated Casey, and if he was sometimes too reckless for his own good, it was seldom deliberate. There were times, when the mood was on him, when he was hard-nosed and stubborn. He had a blunt, good-natured way of talking that often sounded tough to those who didn't know him, but this was usually nothing more than a protective covering with which to confuse those who might otherwise take advantage of him. For it was known all over town that he was a soft touch who had a weakness for lending a hand to those who needed it most.

As his mind enlarged upon the subject, Logan remembered

the many arguments they had had and the trouble they had shared. Without meaning to, he recalled the old radio program which was supposedly based on Casey and his experiences. Some writer friend came up with this idea about doing a series on a newspaper photographer. He had talked Casey into giving him permission to use his name, and because Casey hated to turn a friend down, he had said yes.

The thought of what happened made Logan's smile more noticeable. The program—it was called *Crime Photographer* —had been an unexpected success and had lasted quite a while. Casey had been given a small weekly fee for the use of his name, and he had paid for this in the beginning by taking a concerted ribbing from his colleagues, who used to remind him of the wilder episodes of the program. Casey had protested, not to his colleagues but to the writer. He had even sent letters to say that the character on the radio was a phony and not at all like him. He maintained that the situations dramatized were silly and had no basis in fact, but since there was little percentage in arguing with success, the kidding eventually stopped and Casey collected his royalties, which had been invested with some skill by a broker friend of his. But that was a long time ago and Logan, still grinning at his friend, brought his thoughts back to the moment and told Casey about the gun.

"Stop crying," he said. "If you have to know, I'll tell you. The slug is still in him, but the doctor thinks it's either from a .32 or a .38."

Casey glanced up and his scowl went away. He felt better, a lot better. With the knowledge that Fay Novak's .22 had not killed Alpert, he could tell Logan a little about her and thereby bolster his self-respect. He was about to say so, but Logan continued.

"There was a gun under him."

"Under him?"

"An old .32 Colt automatic."

"You think he tried to use it?"

"It looks that way. We found his permit in his wallet. It

lists two guns—the .32 and a .38 Banker's Special. That one isn't here, and I'm having a man check his apartment to see if he kept it there. The way it looks to us, somebody either marched Alpert in here with a gun and sat him down, and searched the place, or he walked in and caught this someone before he had finished the job. The way he was on the floor behind the desk with that drawer pulled out makes it look as if he had tried to get at the gun and missed."

"When did he get it?"

"It's hard to say," Logan said. "The doc says the wound was fatal—I mean, he couldn't have lived the way he'd been hit, but death wasn't necessarily instantaneous. He might have lived two minutes, five minutes, fifteen minutes. . . . You got any other questions?"

"No, but I've got something to say. I don't think it's important, but I don't want to be accused of holding out."

Logan had walked into the other office to get his hat and coat and now he turned. He rubbed some dust off his brown hat with the sleeve of his jacket, and then he put the hat carefully on his head. He did not say anything, but his eyes were questioning as he waited.

"You couldn't remember Alpert's wife's name," Casey said. "It's Fay Novak. I saw her a couple of hours ago."

"Where?" Logan asked, his eyes opening.

"At the Melody Club."

"You mean you were out with her?"

Casey shook his head. "I was there having a brandy and listening to the guy on the piano when she came in. We said hello and I bought her a drink."

"Then what?"

"We went out." Casey paused while he wondered how much he should tell Logan. When he realized he could give the basic information without lying, he said: "I offered to drive her home and she said no. She said she'd get a cab and she did. I was cruising around thinking about going home when I spotted your radio car."

Logan put on his dark-gray herringbone coat with the fly

front. He buttoned it as he considered what he had heard, and nodded to himself. He said he didn't think Fay Novak was important, but they would pick her up on general principles. He thanked Casey for the information, and when he had locked the office they started along the hall together.

8

THERE WAS no parking space in front of Casey's apartment, but the block was one-way and he found a place diagonally across the street. When he had rolled up the windows, he unlocked the rear deck and took out the camera and equipment bag because he did not like to leave them in the car overnight.

It was quiet here now. There were sporadic traffic sounds on the thoroughfare two blocks away, but here his heels clicked hollowly on the pavement and most of the windows overlooking the street were dark. There was no one in sight as he mounted the worn stone steps of the old, remodeled building and pushed past the outer door, which was never locked. He saw the two men in the dimly lit entryway as the outer door swung behind him, and although their shadowed features did not seem familiar, he noted that one was about his height and weight and the other slender and younger. He also noticed that they waited on opposite sides of the enclosure. As he took his next step, the big man spoke.

"Casey?"

"Yeah."

"Like to talk to you."

"Go ahead."

"Upstairs."

Casey, liking no part of this setup, was thinking fast now and the result produced a sudden feeling of tension and doubt that came out of nowhere. Something about these two reminded him of past experiences that had ended unpleasantly,

and instinct supported the thought that they spelled potential
trouble of one sort or another.

"What's the matter with here?"

He saw the slender youth move as he spoke and knew then
that he had a gun. He had not seen it yet, and there was a
moment when he might have jumped them if his hands had
been free. He thought he could take the big man and he was
willing to back the odds on his companion. The trouble was,
he had the equipment bag slung over one shoulder and the
camera in his other hand. To swing it as a weapon, or even
drop it, was to him unthinkable, and suddenly the moment
was gone and he saw the short-barreled revolver.

"Can you see this?" the slender one said in tight nasal tones.

"I see it."

"My friend says upstairs."

"Unlock the door, Casey," the big man said. "Or give me
the key and I'll do it for you."

He stepped up and took the camera and Casey had to let
it go. He got out his key, a growing annoyance mixing with
the tension. He unlocked the door and concentrated on keeping his muscles loose in case he got another chance to jump
them. He felt the gun jab his spine as he moved inside, and
then they were climbing the stairs in single file, Casey leading.

There were two apartments on the floor and Casey's was on
the right, the living room overlooking the street, the bedroom
at the rear. He unlocked the door and moved aside, but the
gunman was not fooled. He kept his distance, and Casey
moved through the tiny vestibule and turned on a light.

Here, where he could see better, he made a new appraisal
of the pair and knew he had been right the first time. The big
one, who looked to be in his late thirties, wore a blue coat and
a dark-gray hat. Beneath the oddly narrow brim, the broad
face had a swart, muscular look and the brows and the bridge
of his nose were warped by scar tissue. Casey had run up
against the type before. He had never been too worried about
what they could do, and with his second look it seemed to
him that he had seen the fellow somewhere before.

But it was the other man who bothered him and not just because he had the gun. He was skinny and young and bareheaded, and his reddish hair had a greasy look. The mouth was but a slash in the bony face, and the eyes were small and bright and so pale that they seemed almost colorless. The composite picture suggested a disposition that was unpredictable and basically mean, and there was a noticeable nervousness to his movements that was not reassuring.

"Where do you want this?" the big one said, lifting the camera.

Casey told him to put it on the drop-leaf table which stood at one side of the vestibule. He went over and placed the equipment bag on the floor beside it. He got out of his coat, put it on the back of a chair, and set his hat on top of it. He brought forth a cigarette and took his time lighting it.

During this time the big man had been cruising about the room. He moved into the small hall which led to the bath and bedroom. He glanced into the kitchen without entering it and opened the door of the room next to it, which had once been a small dining alcove and was now a compact but complete darkroom.

"All right," Casey said. "Let's get it over with, I'm tired."

"You got some films," the big man said.

"Sure," Casey said. "I've got lots of films."

"These are special ones."

"So?"

"We want them."

Casey looked at him. He looked at the redhead with the gun, and he still did not like what he saw in the pale bright eyes. The tension which had begun to stir downstairs was more noticeable now, and because of what had happened that day he seemed to understand exactly what films they meant. He did not know how they could know about them; he had not the slightest idea who might have sent them. He did understand that they were only errand boys, one with muscle, the other with a gun. The only point in his favor was the fact that he had left Keeler's films safely in Julius Levy's office.

"Have you got any special films in mind?"

"They're in a box, maybe two boxes," the big man said.

"Who says so?"

"We were given the word."

"Then you got it wrong."

"They belonged to a guy named Keeler." The big man tipped one hand. "Let's make it easy, hunh? You've got 'em; we want 'em."

Casey thought it over and realized that there was little point in denying that he knew about Keeler's films. Wherever it had come from, their information was right and he saw no point in arguing about that detail.

"You got part of it right," he said. "Keeler had some films. He left them to me. But they're not here now. They're still in his lawyer's office."

The big man shrugged. "Okay. If that's how you want it, I'll have to take a look."

Casey sat down in the wing chair and watched the fellow look slowly about the room. There was nothing here that could hold any great quantity of negatives except the desk, and as he went over to it, he stopped and gave Casey a warning.

"I want to tell you about my buddy," he said, indicating the redhead with a jerk of his head. "He's a very nervous type. Like if you tried to jump him, the gun would go off, and he's pretty good with it. . . . Watch him, Red," he said. "You know what they told us?" he added. " 'This guy don't like to be pushed around,' they said. 'Sometimes he gets real rough.' "

He glanced at his companion again and said: "If he gets out of the chair, he's yours. Just keep it low, hunh? We don't want to have to go up against the big beef. . . . Do you hear me?"

"I hear you."

"A slug in the leg will stop him just as well. Remember that."

He was already opening a desk drawer as he spoke, and when he found nothing that interested him he went through the little hall and into the bedroom. Casey saw the light go on and heard the drawers being opened and closed. He heard the sound of the closet door, but not until the other came out and started for the darkroom did he have any great concern.

In a way he had the same feeling about his darkroom and equipment and films that Johnny Keeler had about his. The difference was only in degree. Nobody ever entered that dark-room except by invitation, and such invitations were few and far between. Now, knowing what the big man was after, Casey's concern expanded swiftly because, like Keeler, he had also collected over a period of time certain choice negatives that made a pictorial record of his years on the *Express*.

Of little value to anyone but him, he nevertheless treasured them. They had been catalogued carefully in a long, wooden filing case. Right now that case was out in plain sight on top of the paper cabinet, and unless these two had an accurate description of Keeler's two metal film boxes—

The thought was so discouraging he tried to dismiss it. "Take it easy in there," he called to the big man. "That equipment is expensive."

When there was no answer he put his hands on the arms of the chair, but the voice of the redhead stopped him.

"Easy, Buster. You heard what my buddy said."

Casey looked at the gun and then at the face above it and what he saw eliminated all thought of resistance. He had been up against men with guns before. Occasionally, because of carelessness, overconfidence, or inexperience it had been pos-sible to overcome the odds, but this was different and he knew it. The tight fixed smile on the bony face told him that the redhead was potentially dangerous. The pale, compassion-less little eyes confirmed the impression. There had been times in the past when Casey had been perhaps too reckless for his own good, but he was no fool. Right now he was con-vinced that the redhead was just waiting for him to make a move, and he was sufficiently intimidated to sit right where he was.

What he had been afraid of happened a moment later as he watched the big man walk out of the darkroom with the wooden film file, which was about the size of a shoe box. He did not think it would do any good to protest, but he tried.

"Those aren't the films you want," he said. "Those are mine, damn it. You're right about Keeler leaving me some negatives, but they were in two boxes. Metal boxes."

"You could be right," the man said, "but we have to be sure, Casey. If these aren't the ones we want, you'll get them back."

"When?"

"I've got a message for you. Tune in and I'll tell you how it goes." He hesitated, tucking the box under his arm, and a pleased expression on his face. "My party only wants a couple of films. When he gets 'em, that's it. You get the rest back."

"How?" Casey asked, not quite believing this.

"We put the box with the rest of the films in a parcel locker in the South Station. Sometime tomorrow you get the key. Simple, hunh?"

Casey realized that this story might just possibly be true. He wanted to believe it because there was nothing else he could do. He heard the big man speak to the redhead, saw the youth back away. He came slowly to his feet as they reached the doorway, and now the tension and annoyance and apprehension fused in a slow and burning anger that began to churn inside him. From out of this came an idea that he quickly embraced. He could not stop them, but there was something he could do that would perhaps worry them a little. If they told the one who hired them, it might even worry him.

He stood easily now, the confidence growing in him. He saw the redhead back into the vestibule and heard him say if Casey stuck his head into the hall he would pop it off. Then, as the door closed, Casey moved.

Two long steps took him to his camera on the drop-leaf table. Like most experienced press photographers, he kept that camera ready at all times and the focus was pre-set according to individual experience. This particular camera was set at twelve feet because, when the unexpected happened and there were only seconds to get a picture or miss it entirely, such a range had proved to be more effective than any other set focus. If there was time to make a change, the focus could be adjusted; if not, this one had to do.

Now, stopping only long enough to grab the battery for the strobe unit, he jumped toward the two front windows and threw one of them open. He touched the focusing knob without looking at it but knowing that he had added a couple more feet.

He was leaning halfway out the window when the two hoodlums came out of the doorway below and diagonally to the right. He aimed at a square of sidewalk at the bottom of the steps and waited until they reached it. He spoke then, one word crisp and clear.

"Hey!"

That stopped them in their tracks and, knowing at once where the sound had come from, they moved instinctively, turning at the neck, their heads jerking around. The faces were clear in the darkness as they lifted to locate him, and as they did so, he tripped the shutter and light exploded in their eyes.

He took time to give them a sardonic reminder of what he had done. He said: "Thanks," and drew back, not hurrying because he knew the flash would blind them for the next several seconds. There was no sound from below as he pulled the window down, locked it, and drew the shade.

He was chuckling to himself as he moved over to the door and put the chain lock in place. He put the camera on the table and removed the film. Still chuckling, forgetting for the moment that he had perhaps lost a fine collection of negatives, he lifted the roll and kissed it lightly.

He still had no idea who had sent the pair. He was quite sure he had never seen the redhead before, but his companion had seemed vaguely familiar. The picture might help identify him. Such thoughts made him feel immensely better. He was certain the shot he had taken would be a good one, and since he was in no hurry he decided to process the film in the morning. He was on his way to the kitchen for a nightcap when a new and sober thought stopped him.

Tomorrow was Johnny Keeler's funeral. Maybe he should take care of the film and make his prints tonight.

He took this thought with him as he went into the kitchen and made his drink; then, remembering that the services were not until after lunch, he knew there would be plenty of time to take care of the film in the morning.

9

THE CHURCH was full at two o'clock the following afternoon and those who had come to pay their last respects to Johnny Keeler represented a cross section of the city's inhabitants that a poll-taker would have found difficult to classify.

They came from all walks of life, from all faiths. As a class, the newspapers were perhaps best represented. The contingent from the *Express* was lead by Paul Bartholomew, the assistant publisher, and McGrath, the managing editor. All departments were represented, including the pressmen, stereotypers, linotype operators, circulation men, and truck drivers. There were men from the police department, including the deputy commissioner. There were other law officers from the State Police and the District Attorney's office. City Hall was well represented, too, but there were a great many who had no affiliation. These were the taxi drivers, the bartenders, the waiters, the entertainers, many of them women, the small shopkeepers; later, when the eulogy was over, many of them continued on to the cemetery.

It was a subdued and different-looking Casey who stood not far from the grave and listened to the final words. The blue suit and white shirt and black tie gave him a distinguished look, and his thick and often unruly hair remained neatly combed in spite of the cool breeze that still blew steadily in from the sea.

When it was over and the mourners turned away, he moved

quickly to one side, where Alma Jensen had been standing. She was dressed in black now, a half veil shielding her eyes and her pallor from the stares of the curious. On his way to her side, Casey saw Julius Levy and, still watching the woman, stopped to speak to him.

"I want to see you, Julius," he said. "When will you be at your office?"

"I'm going there now."

"Will you be free in half or three quarters of an hour?"

Levy said he would, and Casey continued on until he fell in step with the woman, who was moving slowly toward the road, her head slightly bent. She glanced up as he took her arm and asked if she was all right.

"Yes, Jack. I'm all right."

"Can I give you a ride?" he asked. "There's plenty of room in my car."

"I have a car, thank you."

"Well, isn't there anything I can do?"

"Not now, Jack," she said.

"I didn't mean now," Casey said. "I meant any time."

"You can come and see me." She tightened her arms slightly so that his fingers were compressed against her side. "When you can."

"I will."

"Sometime soon. . . ."

Julius Levy had Keeler's two boxes of negatives on his desk when Casey was shown into his office. His neat dark coat and vest made him look thinner than ever and by contrast gave an added paleness to his delicate features. His eyes were mildly speculative behind the thick glasses, but he waited until Casey was seated before he spoke of the negatives.

"I assumed that you wanted to talk about these."

"Yes," Casey said, "but I haven't made up my mind about that offer. I could use the five grand all right, but Johnny gave me a responsibility. The way things are going, it's bigger than I thought."

He reached into his pocket and brought forth three prints of the film he had made from his front window the night before. By cropping the negative, he had made four-by-five enlargements that showed the two men from the waist up, and the resulting photographs were clear, sharp, and well-lighted. The big man's hat brim masked his face from the forehead up, but his companion, being bareheaded, was completely exposed, and because his face was turned upward in answer to Casey's call, the sharp, bony features were distinct. Now, handing one print to Levy, he told him what had happened.

"Do you know either of them?" he asked.

"No." Levy shook his head. "Have you been to the police?"

"No."

"Why?"

"Because I doubt if it's worth the effort. Suppose I make a complaint and they're picked up. It's their word against mine. There is no assault involved and I can't prove they took my films. Even if I got them booked on some minor charge, they'd be out in an hour."

He leaned forward in his chair, his dark gaze intent. "Whoever hired them probably carries some weight. He has to figure that there's a chance they might be picked up, and that means he's probably got a mouthpiece ready to put up bail. If they skip and forfeit bail—he might even tell 'em to—it wouldn't matter. Unless the cops could make them talk, which I doubt like hell, all I'd wind up with is a run-around."

"You're going to drop the matter?"

"Not by a damn sight. I'm going to try to find out who sent them. I don't think the police can do it, but maybe I know someone who can. But the reason I'm telling you all this is this: I can't let go of those negatives now for five thousand or fifty."

He grunted softly and said: "A private dick named Clem Alpert who might have been in the position to do some blackmailing—he has probably done it before—was murdered last night."

"I read about it."

"He was at Keeler's place Saturday night," Casey said and went on to explain his thoughts about the unlocked safe. "If my theory is right, while Keeler was lying there unconscious Alpert got hold of something that must have been very important. Somebody wanted that something enough to kill for it."

"I agree."

"Someone sent those two hoods to my place for the same reason. It might even be the same person if he missed with Alpert because they didn't try me until two or three hours after Alpert got hit. So how can I be sure this client of yours—"

"Not client." Levy made the correction politely. "I merely agreed to act as a—shall we say, intermediary."

"All right, intermediary," Casey said. "I know your reputation and I know you wouldn't waste time being even an intermediary for riffraff. But I've got things on my mind, Julius. I'm afraid to let any one man look over those negatives and pick out what he wants. I have to know who wants a negative and why before I can make up my mind. Even then, the answer may be no. I don't know if I'm getting across to you, but—"

"I understand perfectly," Levy said. "Unfortunately I can't identify those who want the negatives at this time."

"Those? There's more than one?"

"There are three, to be exact."

"And they all want the same film, or films?"

"That's right."

"Then that offer of the five thousand is a joint offer."

Casey leaned back in his chair, his scowl deepening. He looked at Levy and glanced at the film boxes, and somehow he was more confused than ever.

"Do you know all three guys personally?"

"I do. And I can say this much. All have enviable reputations, all are high-placed."

"Could any one of them, acting individually, have hired those two punks who came to my place last night?"

"I would say no. Emphatically no."

Casey believed the lawyer, but he also recalled Johnny Keeler's letter and his words of caution. It was obvious now that some of the negatives spelled trouble for certain people, and such knowledge weighed heavily upon him.

"Can you get in touch with any or all of these people?"

"I think so."

"All right then, tell them this. Maybe I'm being stubborn, maybe I'm too cautious; maybe I'm afraid, but I'm not going to hand over any of those negatives until I'm convinced that nobody will get hurt. I haven't any complex like Johnny had about letting go of a negative, but I can't do it unless I know who wants those negatives and why. If these three guys don't know me, you'll have to give me a character reference, but before I hand over films to anybody, I have to know who I'm dealing with. I'll meet with them, face to face, whenever they say. What they tell me will be held in strict confidence. When I know what the score is, maybe I'll agree to the proposition and maybe I won't, but that's the best I can do."

Levy made no reply. In place of words he made a gesture with both hands as Casey rose and reached for his hat and coat. When he had them on, he stepped to the desk and picked up the two metal boxes.

"I'll take these now," he said. "If they cause any more trouble, I'm liable to burn the whole damn business. If I do, I'll let you know."

Casey drove directly to his apartment from Levy's office, and when he had parked his car near the entrance he sat a moment to study the street and the cars that were parked there. Satisfied that no one was watching him, he got out and hurried up the steps and unlocked the inner door. Once inside, he bypassed the stairs and moved to a door that opened under the first flight. A wall switch there brought light from the bulb over the landing, and this showed him the way down the dusty stairs to the cement floor below. After that, he had to grope for a string, which activated another bulb in the ceiling, before he could find his way to the row of ceiling-high cages which had been set against one wall.

There were six of these, constructed of two-by-fours and chicken wire and allotted to the tenants to provide them with storage space for things their apartments could not accommodate. Each had a padlock, and Casey unfastened his. Then he stepped inside, where he kept a wardrobe trunk, a foot locker, a B-4 bag, a seldom-used suitcase, and assorted odds and ends. A piece of discarded canvas helped to keep out the dust, and he lifted this long enough to put the two film boxes on the foot locker. After he pulled the canvas back, he snapped the padlock in place and went upstairs. He did not stop at his apartment but went directly to his car and drove to the office. He was in the hall on his way to the studio when Lanvin, coming out, met him.

"You've got a visitor," he said.

"What does he want?"

"It's not a he, it's a dame."

"What kind of a dame?" Casey asked, surprised by the announcement because female visitors to the studio were practically unknown.

"Not bad."

"Well, what does she want?"

"She wants to see you," Lanvin said and went on his way.

Sheila Garrett was sitting in a chair by Casey's desk. She had changed her clothes since the funeral and now wore a navy-blue dress and a black cloth coat. In that first instant, her small oval face held an expression that could have come from some inner annoyance, or possibly from boredom, but when she saw him it vanished and the dark eyes looked relieved. She came to her feet and said hello, and Casey said hello and asked if she had been waiting long.

"Not too long. They told me they didn't know when you would be in, but I decided to wait a while anyway. . . . Is there some place we could talk?"

Cleary, who had been sitting in the corner pretending to

read a paperback book, stood up. "I can go out and get a cup of coffee," he said hopefully.

Casey thought it over and shook his head. There was bound to be some traffic in and out of the office, and at best it was hardly the place for a private conversation.

"Sit still. . . . We'll find a place," he said to the girl and then, taking her arm, he led her into the hall and out to the elevator.

They rode up one floor, but instead of going into the city room proper, he turned into a corridor which contained the small private offices of some of the specialists. A glance at his watch told him it was a few minutes after five and this prompted him to try the financial editor's room. His guess was right, and as Sheila sat down, he closed the door and eased into the chair behind the desk. She took the cigarette he offered and leaned forward to accept a light. She inhaled as she settled back, opening her coat and pushing it back as she crossed her knees.

"I've been doing a lot of thinking since this morning," she said finally. "I guess I never realized how popular my father was or how many friends he had."

Casey, finding no appropriate comment, nodded in agreement.

"I'm afraid I was never a very devoted daughter," she continued. "We were never very close. I never knew quite how to take him."

"He was a great guy," Casey said, "but not always too easy to get along with."

"I didn't even try to understand him. Of course, always living with my mother, I only got her side of the story. Even when I was little, I hardly ever saw him. Then, since I've been married, things were even worse." She studied the end of her cigarette, glanced around for some receptacle, and tapped the ash on the floor. "Now that it's too late, I feel very guilty about my lack of understanding. I know there is not too broad a line between sentiment and sentimentality, but the more I thought about him the more I realized that I didn't have a single thing of his that I wanted to keep. There's nothing at the hotel he cared about or anything that would be worth saving, and that's why I decided to come and ask you about those films he left."

Casey looked at her with one eye and then with both. He thought: *Oh, Lord, here we go again,* and the unexpectedness of her words made him mute so that he could only look at her until she continued.

"They're not valuable, are they?"

"Valuable?"

"I mean, if you can get a lot of money for them, I wouldn't think of asking you to give them to me."

She said this with great innocence, and if Casey had not already been aware of the trouble inherent in those films, he might have believed her.

"I don't think they're that valuable," he said. "There might be a few that you could sell for a buck or two to some magazine or newspaper."

"Well, then, could I have them?"

"All of them?"

"Yes, if you don't mind."

Casey put his cigarette out and leaned back, his dark gaze somber as it moved beyond her and focused on the door. He could not quarrel with the words he had heard. The phrases were proper and correct. The request was simple, direct, and made with almost too much confidence. Under some circumstances it would be difficult to explain this, but he had no such compunction now because a thread of skepticism was mingling with his thoughts. The background of Keeler's relationship with his daughter was well known to him, and he was not ready to believe that what he had heard was the complete truth. Even so, he found it difficult to come out with an arbitrary refusal.

"You'd like to take them home and keep them," he said. "So you can look at them from time to time, as a reminder of some of the things your father had done."

"I suppose so."

"Sort of like a family album?"

"Something like that."

He hesitated again, sensing a slight change in her inflection, as though she thought such questioning was somewhat presumptuous. He saw no point in going into details about the trouble those negatives had already caused, but he did mention the letter Johnny Keeler had left for him and gave her its substance.

"I'm sorry," he said. "If you think this makes me a heel, I plead guilty. But I don't see how I can turn those films over to anyone just now. If he hadn't wanted me to be careful about what happened to them, he wouldn't have bothered to write that letter."

"Oh." She sat up, drawing the coat about her, her mouth tightening a little as the annoyance began to show. "But I told you why I wanted them. Are you suggesting that I might use some of those films to make trouble for anyone?"

"I'm not suggesting anything."

"You most certainly are."

"If it's important to you," Casey said, not wanting to sound as if he was quibbling, "maybe I can go through those boxes later on and pick out—"

"That isn't the same thing," she cut in icily. "This is a matter of sentiment to me and I had hoped you'd understand. I should think that if you were such a good friend of my father's you might respect his daughter's wishes."

"I'd like to," Casey said evenly. "I can understand your viewpoint all right, but right now I feel I'm more obligated to your father than I am to you. I don't think he'd want me to give you those films at this time, and it's his wishes I'm thinking about. If your sentiment is genuine, it certainly should last another week or so until I can go through those negatives. Once I know what's in those boxes, you'll be welcome to what's in them—at least to most of it."

She rose abruptly as he finished, the haughty look he had noticed in Levy's office taking command of her face again. She seemed about to say something else in the same vein and then, as though prompted by some inner impulse, there was a slight transformation in her face and her tone was more controlled.

"I don't suppose you would consider letting me borrow them now so I could pick out the ones I wanted?"

"I'm sorry. Maybe later if I—"

"Never mind," she interrupted stiffly. "I should have known better than to expect any consideration or understanding from a newspaper photographer." She jerked the door open and glared at him. "Which way is the elevator?"

Casey said he would show her. He led the way along the corridor, made the turn, came to the foyer. He pushed the button for her and waited until the car started down. He was not pleased with his performance and regretted what he had to do, but at the same time he was convinced that he had made the only decision possible under the circumstances. Then, as his thoughts moved on, he remembered something else he wanted to do and started off in search of a telephone.

10

IT WAS nearly six o'clock when Casey turned on Washington Street and entered the foyer of a four-story office building just around the corner. The single elevator was newer than the building and had been switched to automatic at this hour so he rode to the third floor and went along the hall to the last door on the left. The lettering on the panel said Samuel Delemater. There was nothing here or in the ante-room beyond which gave any indication of the manner of business that might be transacted here, but Casey knew Delemater as one of the best and most dependable private detectives in town.

A doorway to the adjacent office stood open and Casey paused there, his rugged face warping in a slow grin as he glanced about and focused on the man behind the desk. The office itself had a cluttered, untidy look and its furnishings—the two chairs, the filing cabinet, the water cooler, and the bookcase, which held more magazines and papers than it did books—looked as if they had never been new. But if the office was cluttered, the desk was more so. It had been moved diagonally across one corner so that the light from the lone window was of some use to the occupant of the chair, and the flat top bore testimony to one of Delemater's main interests in life.

He was on the telephone at the moment, one elbow propped on the desk, his hat on the back of his head and a worried look on his solidly rounded face. He seemed to be listening intently and making notes on a piece of paper with a pencil he held in his other hand. When he recognized his caller, he invited him in with a jerk of his head. As Casey advanced, he saw that a *Racing Form,* a *Morning Telegraph,* and a *Scratch Sheet* were spread out before him.

Sheets of copy paper covered with penciled calculations were interspersed with the other papers. A glass ash tray was filled to overflowing, and on Delemater's left were a pitcher of water, a tin of bicarbonate of soda, a glass, and a spoon. On the other end of the desk were a half-filled bottle of bourbon and a glass, which was at the moment empty.

Casey's grin broadened as he listened to Delemater say: "Yeah . . . yeah . . . yeah. . . ." Each time he spoke, he wrote something down in the margin of the *Racing Form.* Finally he nodded absently and said: "Eight minutes, hunh? Okay, I'll call you back. I want to listen to it."

He cradled the telephone, leaned back. "Hi," he said.

"For God's sake," Casey said. "Don't tell me they're running somewhere at this hour."

"What do you mean, this hour?" Delemater scoffed. "Didn't anyone ever tell you about time zones? Hell, they're going strong on the west coast. I think I've got something good going in the fourth at Tanforan. You want to get a bet down?"

Here." He pushed the open *Racing Form* toward Casey. "Sit down. Pick one. Let's see how good you are."

Casey stepped over to the water cooler. There was a paper-cup dispenser fastened to the wall, and he clicked out two cups and made a nest of them. He filled them partway with water, came back to the desk, and added some bourbon. When he had sampled the brew and found it would do, he took off his coat and sat down across the desk from Delemater.

"The fourth at Tanforan?" he said. "Who do you like?"

"*Azure Blue,*" Delemater said happily. "In a breeze. You got about five minutes."

Casey took the *Racing Form,* reversed it, and began to study the race Delemater had mentioned. His first glance told him there were nine starters. Beside each one there were three tiny sets of figures, apparently indicating the odds at various times.

"Any scratches?"

"No."

"The outside figures the morning line?"

"Yep."

Casey pushed his hat back and reached for a pencil, attentive now and forgetting for the moment why he had come. Because there was not much time, he eliminated the four longest shots and concentrated on the others, checking the weights, past performances, the order of finishes in recent races.

This one was an allowance race at a mile and one-sixteenth for four-year-olds and upwards with a three-thousand-dollar purse, and he soon found two horses that looked like co-favorites. Delemater's penciled figures confirmed this, and because Casey did not like the price, he gave his attention to the three remaining entries. He soon settled on one and began to concentrate as he checked the record with the others who seemed to have a chance.

The horse's name was *Overhead* and his last few outings were discouraging. In his five most recent starts he'd finished far back, except for his last race, when he had come in fourth.

But he'd won two good races in the fall of the previous year and on paper he seemed to have more class than the others. Also, in running down the last race, Casey saw something that caught his interest. The distance then had been a mile and *Overhead* must have been left practically at the post since he not only started last but was still in that position in the back stretch. Even so, he had finished a close fourth and now, carrying three pounds less, with a sixteenth of a mile farther to go and at prices that had varied from the morning line of 7–1 to 9–2, he seemed worth a small bet.

"Hurry up," Delemater said.

"I am." Casey tossed the paper back to the detective. "*Overhead.*"

"*Overhead?*" Delemater eyed him skeptically. He scoffed openly, but in spite of this reaction, his suspicions were aroused and he bent over to examine the sheet. "Let me see. . . . Hmm . . . Hah." He glanced up and grinned.

"Are you nuts? He ain't won a race this year. He ain't even been close."

"He won more dough last year than *Azure Blue.*"

"That was last year. He hasn't been in front since last fall."

Casey was grinning by this time, not because of the situation but because he always got a kick out of Delemater, who played the horses with a dedication that a stock analyst gave to a company balance sheet.

"Maybe he's sick," he said, knowing he'd get a rise.

"Sick, hell," Delemater said. "He's ready for the glue factory."

The telephone rang before he could elaborate and he snatched it up.

"Yeah," he said. "Yep. . . . Any changes? No, hunh? Give me ten win and ten show on *Azure Blue*. And wait a minute." He cupped the mouthpiece with his hand. "They're at the post," he said. "You kidding about *Overhead?*"

Casey said no. He said if the horse was ready and the stable was trying, *Overhead* could take it all.

"At nine to two," he added, "he's worth a ride. Five to win."

Delemater found the selection absurd. "Hell, I ought to book that one myself."

"Okay." Casey tossed a five-dollar bill on the desk. "Book it."

Delemater sighed, hesitated, and was tempted, but in the end his courage oozed away. "And Charlie," he said into the mouthpiece. "Five more on *Overhead* to win. Yeah. And I want to hear it, okay?"

He wedged the telephone against his ear with a hunched shoulder to free both hands, and now he opened the tin of bicarbonate of soda and spooned a little into a glass. He added water and stirred vigorously. When he had tossed off the mixture, he put the glass down, took the phone in his right hand, and waited expectantly. About ten seconds later he belched loudly, and with this out of the way, he reached to his right, poured a little bourbon into a second glass, added water, and took a swallow. He leaned back in the swivel chair and began to teeter gently back and forth, a contented smile on his face as he waited.

"They're having a little trouble at the starting gate with *Shan Pal*," he said. Then, his eyes opening as he stopped teetering, he said: "They're off!"

He leaned forward then, pencil in hand, as he relayed the calls that came to him. "*Azure Blue*—by God, he broke on top —*Prime Selection, Shan Pal, Georgia Girl.*"

He began to hum softly as he waited for the next call. "Dum-dum-dedum. . . . In the turn—*Azure Blue, Prime Selection, Shan Pal, Georgia Girl.* . . .

"In the backstretch it's *Azure Blue*—stick in there, baby— *Shan Pal, Prime Selection, Georgia Girl.*" He glanced up to grin at Casey. "What happened to *Overhead?*"

"He comes from behind," Casey said.

"Yeah, I'll bet. . . . Into the far turn it's *Azure Blue* by one, *Shan Pal* by one, *Georgia Girl* by one-and-a-half, *Prime Selection*—he must have folded—by a half. . . .

"Coming into the stretch it's still *Azure Blue* by one. *Georgia Girl* by a half, *Silver Sword* by a head, and *Night Train.*"

He put his pencil down, the telephone tight against his ear and every nerve attentive as he waited for the winner.

"Here we are," he said. "Coming up now."

Then, before he could continue, something happened to his face. His gray eyes jerked wide open and his mouth sagged. He seemed to have trouble breathing and his voice, when it came, was shocked and incredulous.

"Overhead?"

It was not a statement; it was a question.

"Overhead?" he said again in awed tones. "How the hell did he get in there?"

He did not give the other results but hung up slowly, his expression dazed as Casey began to laugh. Like a man who had just received a mortal blow, he shook his head as if to ward off the aftereffects of the injury. He reached for his glass, finished the drink in one gulp, and put it down hard.

"How do you like that? Jesus, he never even got a call."

"I told you," Casey said. "He's a stretch runner. . . . What about *Azure Blue?*"

"He ran third."

"You might break even," Casey said by way of consolation.

"I doubt it," Delemater said. "Boy, am I glad I didn't take your bet myself. . . . Oh, well," he added, with the easy philosophy of all horse players. "You can't win 'em all. I got a good run for my money anyway."

He made another small drink, swirled it around in the glass, and tossed it off in one continuous motion. Then, having recovered his composure, he dialed a number.

"Have you got the prices yet?" he asked presently. "Yeah." He picked up his pencil and began to jot down some figures. "Yeah. . . . Okay, Charlie, thanks. I'll call you later." He hung up, sighed, and gave Casey a quick, envious glance as he reached for his wallet. "You're some handicapper, kid. *Overhead* paid twelve twenty."

"What about *Azure Blue?*"

"Not too bad. Three sixty to show. That means I only lose two bucks."

He used the pencil again and did a quick calculation. Casey's five-dollar bill was still on the desk so Delemater pushed it toward him, took twenty-five dollars from his wallet and added it to the five; then, digging into a trouser's pocket, he produced a fifty-cent piece.

"You don't have to pay me now," Casey said.

"Why not? I'll collect from Charlie. Who knows when I'll see you again. Take it and quit while you're ahead."

"I'm going to," Casey said as he picked up the money. "And so are you, for today."

As he spoke, he began to collect all the papers on Delemater's desk and the detective watched him a moment, not quite understanding what this was all about. As Casey pulled the papers toward him, he protested.

"Wait a minute. I'm not through—"

"You are for now, Sam," Casey said. "It's time to get to work. Do you still get forty bucks a day?"

Delemater watched Casey fold all the papers and anchor them with the bourbon bottle. Finally, as though aware that further protest would be useless, he said:

"Forty-five."

"How come?"

"Inflation. The cost-of-living index is still rising. Or haven't you read the papers lately? . . . Plus expenses. What do I have to do?"

"Find a couple of guys for me."

"For you, or for the *Express?*"

Casey thought it over and said he wasn't sure. "If anything comes out of it the paper can use, I can stick them. If not I'll pay you." He reached into his pocket and took out the photograph of the two men who had come calling on him the night before. "Do you know them?"

Delemater accepted the picture, glanced at it, then put it on the desk. He sat a moment and then, as though some more important thought had occurred to him, he pushed the chair back and stood up. He took Casey's empty paper cup and dropped it in the wastebasket. He took the two glasses, the tin of bicarbonate of soda, and the spoon and moved over to put them in the medicine cabinet, which stood above the washbowl. Casey watched him silently, and was reminded again that if anyone could help him Sam Delemater was probably the man.

For Delemater, who was about his age, had been a cop for quite a while, and a good one. He had been made a plainclothes man while quite young and not long after that he had been promoted to detective. That he had never reached the next rung in the ladder of promotion was due chiefly to his lack of diplomacy. He called his shots as he saw them and he made his arrests the same way. He had never been impressed by names, social position, or political influence, and when he finally realized that he could not do the job the way he thought it should be done without interference from above, he had resigned and taken a job with a national agency that had a branch office in town.

Two or three years of this had qualified him as an all-around operator and he had eventually set up his own business. Being his own boss suited him because he was essentially a lone wolf. He had tried marriage once, but it had not worked out, and since then he had gone his own way, always making enough to get by and indulging himself when he felt like it in the three things that interested him most, which were horses, women, and whisky, in that order.

There was nothing very distinguished about his appearance or his looks. He paid very little attention to clothes and no one had ever told him he was well groomed. He was not much more than average height, and stocky, but he had no paunch and he could move very fast when he had to. His round face normally carried a bland expression and only the alert and watchful gray eyes warned the more observant that here, when the occasion demanded, was a hard and uncompromising individual. Now, remembering all this, Casey knew that if Delemater agreed to help he would do so with a persistent and tenacious application to the job which usually paid off.

"So how about it?" he said when the detective sat down.

Delemater again considered the photograph. "The bareheaded one I've never seen," he said. "The other one I think I have but I don't know where." He glanced up, one brow crooked. "Why are you coming to me? You know more people around town than I do. You've got plenty of pigeons."

"Maybe." Casey grinned at him. "But you've got different kinds of pigeons, Sam. On a thing like this your pigeons should be better."

"You could be right," Delemater said, "but my pigeons don't work for love. They've generally got their little hands out. That's where the expense money comes in."

"Sure. Just keep it down if you can."

"All right. Fill me in. What's your interest in these two?"

Casey told him, but he gave no more details than were necessary to round out the picture. Delemater listened thoughtfully, nodding his head imperceptibly from time to time as he absorbed the information. He said he had heard something about Johnny Keeler's negatives.

"I used to go up to his place once in a while," he said. "I've seen him take those pictures."

"There's just an outside chance," Casey said, "that a colleague of yours got too interested in the same thing."

"What colleague?"

"Clem Alpert."

"Some colleague," Delemater said with quick disdain. "That guy was too greedy to be smart. I never wished him any bad luck but knowing the kind of jobs he took I can't cry too much. I would rather have set him up so the commissioner could lift his license than pick a three-horse parlay. . . . If I locate these two lads I call you, right?"

Casey said yes. He said if he wasn't home to call the office and if he wasn't there to tell the city editor to try and locate him on the company radio. He stood up, adjusted his hat, and put on his coat. Delemater watched him, but when he saw Casey pick up the collection of papers he had folded, he uttered a protest of quick alarm.

"Wait a minute. Where are you going with those?"

"Out," said Casey. "If I leave this stuff you'll keep right on playing the horses."

"No, I won't."

"I want you to go to work on this now."

"I will." Delemater grinned and held his right hand up, palm upward. "Scout's honor."

Casey could not help laughing, and as he hesitated, Delemater continued.

"I have to eat dinner, don't I?" he asked plaintively. "And I have to have something to read while I eat. I have to figure out how I did for the day."

He might have said more, but the telephone rang just then and he reached for it. He spoke, listened, looked up at Casey, and said: "Yeah, right here. . . . For you."

That the call should be for him did not surprise Casey. He had left word at the studio that he was coming here before he went to dinner and he assumed that this was a business call. He knew he was wrong when he said hello because the voice that came to him was both enigmatic and unfamiliar.

"Casey? . . . I understand you want to do some talking about that offer Julius Levy made."

It took Casey a moment to understand what was meant, to recall the things he had said to the lawyer. Before he could reply the voice continued.

"I believe you said you wanted to meet the three men who made that offer."

"That's right."

"Very well. We have arranged for you to do so. Have you got a pencil there? . . . Write down this address."

Casey did so and was aware that the location was a select one just off Beacon on the river.

"Apartment 6," the voice said. "When can you make it?"

"Ten minutes," Casey said. "Maybe fifteen."

"Very good. We'll expect you."

He hung up slowly, his brow grooved and his dark eyes full of thought. He glanced at Delemater but saw no reason to confide in him. He said to get busy and that he'd be seeing him; then he wheeled and left the room.

11

THE APARTMENT HOUSE that Casey sought was a six-story building and looked expensive. A marquee extended from the elaborate entrance to the curb, and beneath it was a rubber mat with the number blocked on it in white against a darker background. There was a yellow no-parking line at the curb, too, but Casey pulled up as far as he could and from the glove compartment took out a card which said PRESS and propped it against the windshield. Sometimes this helped and sometimes, if the cop on the beat wasn't feeling well, it didn't. And since he did not expect to stay long, he decided to take a chance and now he walked through the foyer and into the lobby, seeing the uniformed employee behind the desk and switchboard and the second man in a similar uniform standing beyond the elevator.

They gave him a slow and searching look, but because he still wore the clothes he had put on for the funeral, his appearance was both well groomed and impressive, and he was not questioned as he stepped into the elevator and said: "Six, please."

When the elevator stopped and he stepped out he saw at once that there was but one apartment to the floor. The foyer here had a long marble-topped table flanked by two tapestried chairs and backed by a large, gilt-framed mirror. As he pressed the button recessed in the side of the door, he recalled again Julius Levy's words when he said the offer had been made by high-placed people and he decided that the lawyer could have added one other word—rich. He was still speculating when the inner door swung open to frame a straight-standing, elderly man somberly clad in gray trousers and a dark jacket.

"Mr. Casey?"

He stood back and Casey entered. When the door closed the man made a tentative gesture with one hand and Casey understood that he was to leave his hat and coat. As he turned, he got a glimpse through a doorway on his left of a large, picture-book living room. With Casey's hat and coat in his care, the man said: "That way, sir. The first door on your left, if you please."

Casey took a breath and moved to the right down a carpeted hall to the proper doorway, and as he turned and stepped across the threshold, he found himself in a squarish, pine-paneled room. He had a vague impression of leather uphol-stered chairs and a divan, walls of books, and the glowing logs in the fireplace. Then, as he identified the three men who were waiting in front of it, he knew Julius Levy's esti-mate had been no exaggeration.

If it had been necessary for Casey to photograph the trio, he would have posed them as they stood, with the big man in the center, the lean-looking one on the left, and the shorter, wiry man on the right. The mental caption he made up as he identified them was of the usual left to right fashion and read: Congressman Frederick Babcock, Broker Donald Caldwell, District Attorney T. J. (Tim) Eagan. It was Caldwell who stepped forward and acted the host.

He shook hands and said: "You know Fred Babcock and Tim Eagan." He paused to let Casey say he did; then added: "It was good of you to come. What are you drinking? Or would you prefer to fix your own?"

He waved to a well-stocked bar wagon and Casey thanked him and stepped up to sample its wares. He poured some ten-year-old bourbon into an old-fashioned glass, ignored the sil-ver tongs and took an ice cube from the container with his fingers, added water from a silver pitcher. He said: "Cheers," and when they nodded he took a swallow.

"I thought this would be a good place to talk," Caldwell

said. "The family is out and we won't be disturbed. Shall we sit down and get comfortable?"

He sat down on the red-leather divan and Eagan joined him. Babcock took one of the matching chairs and Casey took the other. He busied himself lighting a cigarette to give himself a moment to think, and he was more confused than ever now because he could not imagine any photograph Johnny Keeler had ever taken that would cause these three men any concern.

They were about the same age and Casey knew they had been classmates in college. Babcock, who had a rangy build and a serious, long-jawed face, was a lawyer and, since the last election, a freshman congressman from this district. Caldwell had more bulk, and although he was prematurely bald, he was more handsome than the others and both his unlined face and the top of his head had a rich man's tan that came from southern sunshine and not from a sun lamp. Eagan, with his sharp features, short-cropped hair, and broad-rimmed glasses had a gamecock look, and his record substantiated this gameness.

"Well—" Caldwell took some of his drink and glanced at his companions. "Do you want to carry the puck, Tim?" he asked.

Eagan cleared his throat and made the direct approach. "Julius Levy says you're holding out because you're afraid some of Keeler's film might get into the wrong hands, right?"

"Right."

"And how do we stack up?"

"Fine."

"Then what's the problem? I don't think it's money because from what I've heard about you you're not that kind of guy."

Casey thought it over and found that Eagan was a hard man to answer. He had the feeling that he was being shoved into a corner, and he sought a reasonable explanation that would not seem unduly pig-headed or stubborn. After a moment he came up with one.

"Keeler knew better than anyone," he said, "that some of

his old negatives could make trouble for certain people. He knew he should have destroyed them, but he'd built up a complex over the years and simply couldn't make himself do it. He left a letter for me with those films," he added, and went on to give some of its thoughts.

"I don't like the responsibility, but I've got it and I'm stuck with it. Since yesterday I've learned that some other people are pretty damn interested in those films, so where do I draw the line?"

"How do you mean?" Babcock said.

"I mean, how do I make up my mind who's to get a crack at those films and who isn't?"

He let them chew on that a moment and then said: "The way I see it is that since those films are mine I have the responsibility. I also have to call the shots. Even if you give me all the answers I won't promise to give you what you want, but I can tell you this. A, you either trust me to keep a confidence or you don't—"

"Certainly we trust you," Eagan said.

"And b," Casey added, "unless you can tell me what the pictures are and why you are afraid of them, the best I can do is thank Mr. Caldwell for this drink and cut out."

This statement brought a noticeable silence as each man considered its implication. Casey had spoken quietly and without aggressive overtones, but his ultimatum was no less effective. It was also obvious that they were not used to being talked to like this. But they were intelligent, well-brought-up gentlemen and they had been taught to face facts. Again it was Caldwell who broke the ice.

"What the hell," he said. "He's got a point. So come on, Tim. Let's level with him."

"Okay." Eagan put his glass on an end table and leaned back on the divan. "This may take a while, Casey," he said, "but I'll keep it as short as I can. To get the picture I have to go back more than twenty years to a party Keeler gave for us. By us I mean the university hockey team. We all played on it as seniors. We had a good season and Keeler was a hockey buff so he asked us all up one Saturday night after the season was over. Were you ever up there at that suite of his in the Avon when he brought over some girl from the burlesque show to put on a little act?"

Casey said yes. He said he'd been talking about the same thing with someone from the paper the other day. He said he understood how Keeler got the girls to come to his place and he knew the house rules.

"That makes it easier," Eagan said. "You've been there so you know the routine. But for us it was a big deal. We were probably twenty-one or twenty-two years old and getting ready to go to graduate school and we hadn't seen anything like this before. For us this was really living it up and we knew it would give us something to talk about for a long time to come."

He hesitated, a suggestion of a smile touching his mouth as though he was reliving that night and still finding some humor in it.

"We'd had a little too much to drink, of course," he said, "but we were behaving ourselves and watching the act, some of us standing, some sitting. Well, I guess the girl herself had maybe one drink too many. She was really enjoying herself and she had stripped down almost to the buff when she swirled around and came up between Don and Fred." He nodded at Caldwell and Babcock. "She pushed between them and draped her arms around their shoulders, and just then a flashbulb exploded in the room. When we could see again Keeler was chuckling and getting ready to take another picture."

He reached for his glass and drained it. "That got a big laugh from everybody, and it must have encouraged the girl because she kept on moving, still dancing, and spun around and plopped herself right down on my lap. She was only there five seconds but it was long enough for Keeler to get another picture." He grunted softly. "I thought about that picture when I saw the one years ago of the midget on J. P. Morgan's lap at some congressional investigation.

"Keeler took perhaps another four or five pictures that night, and naturally we got a kick out of the whole thing. A couple of days later he gave us each a print of the photograph and we had a fine time showing them to anybody who'd look at them and bragging about what big shots we were." He lifted one hand idly and let it fall back on his thigh. "Well, we finished graduate school and went off to war. Maybe once in five years we'd get together and happen to think of that night and reminisce a bit. It wasn't until last year that we began to worry about those two films and realize that they could just possibly cause each one of us one hell of a lot of grief."

He stood up and went over to the bar wagon to make a fresh drink. Caldwell, seeing that Casey's glass was empty, stepped up and took it away from him. He said: "Bourbon, wasn't it?" And Casey said: "Yes," and waited until the drinks were made and the others were seated.

"Why?" he asked. "I mean, what happened that gave you the idea those films were dangerous to you?"

"We got the idea that someone wanted to use them," Babcock said.

"Let's go back a minute," Eagan said. "What did you mean, Casey, when you said that yesterday you found some other people were pretty damn interested in those films?"

Casey told him. He spoke of Clem Alpert, adding that although he had no proof, there was a possibility that Alpert might have been involved. He told about the two hoodlums who had come to his place the previous night.

"This afternoon," he said, "Sheila Garrett came to the office and made a pitch for them."

"You didn't give them to her?" Eagan asked quickly.

"No," Casey said. "She gave me a story about wanting them for sentimental reasons, but somehow, after what happened last night, I wasn't exactly convinced. Even if I had been, I wouldn't have let them out of my hands right now. I told her so." He paused and looked from one to the other. "What you're saying is that someone's out to get all three of you. Who?"

Again there was a moment of indecision while the three men exchanged glances. Caldwell shrugged and Babcock gave a small nod of his head and finally Eagan said:

"John Flynn."

"Big John Flynn? Of Flynn Enterprises?" Again Casey paused while he sought some explanation. When none came to him, he said: "Is this a guess or—"

"It's a little more than a guess," Caldwell said.

"How would he even know about those films?"

"You haven't been listening, Casey," Eagen said. "I said that party was for the hockey team. Flynn was a classmate and he played hockey, too. The four of us made up two thirds of that team. Flynn was there when those pictures were taken."

"But what has he got against you?"

"Several things," Caldwell said, "but they're all in his mind. . . . This is going to take a while, too," he added. "Are you sure you want to hear it?"

"It's up to you," Casey said.

"We were all friends in college," Eagan said. "Fred and I went on to law school and Don went to business school. Flynn went to work. About that time he was having some dates with Don's sister." He glanced at Caldwell. "Why don't you tell him?"

"Without going into a lot of detail," Caldwell said, "I guess he fell in love with my sister. He wanted to marry her, and she turned him down and he blamed me. I think what made it worse was that his own marriage did not turn out too well and he's been building up a grudge against me ever since."

He bunched his lips and said: "Actually, I had nothing to do with it. I introduced him in the first place and I had him around the house a few times. I didn't pay much attention to what went on between him and my sister one way or the other. To be truthful, I think my father didn't care too much for the idea. He sent Ann off to Europe, and when she came

back she didn't see much of Flynn. He told me to my face
that it was my fault. He had some kind of persecution complex and said I fixed it for him because I didn't want an Irish
Catholic for a brother-in-law."

"Which was utter nonsense, on the face of it," Eagan said.
"Because I'm just as much an Irish Catholic as Flynn—a
better one probably—and Don's sister married a cousin of
mine. I told Flynn so one day and that made him sore at me.
There was one other thing, but Fred knows more about that
and he can tell you better than I can."

"Flynn wanted to get into the City Club," Babcock said.
"We were all members and I was on the committee on ad-
missions. He came to me and asked me to put him up. I told
him I couldn't. The rules are clear on that point, and I explained that he would have to get two members to write a
letter and after that we could act on his application. He got
real sore about it, but he finally got the two letters. Then he
was turned down. He's never forgotten it and he's never
forgiven me in spite of the fact that I wasn't the one who
blackballed him."

"He waited a long time," Casey said. "I mean, if you're
right about those films."

"I think he's had a lot of hate building up for us over the
years," Eagan said. "But it's only since he's been the power
behind the throne in politics that he started to let us know it.
He can be a very tough battler and he's an expert at in-
fighting."

"I beat his man for the House seat in the last election,"
Babcock said. "I'm running again in the fall and I know it
will be close. A picture like that—me with my arm around a
practically naked show girl—even one taken twenty years
ago, could make the difference."

"No magazine or newspaper would dare publish it," Casey
said.

"No reputable one," Eagan corrected. "There are fly-by-
night magazines that publish one issue and fold and nobody
can find them. But such a picture wouldn't have to be pub-

lished, Casey. There's no law to prevent you from making a
hundred prints, for instance, and handing them out to your
friends. I doubt if a court would hold such a picture porno-
graphic, so you could hand the picture to a friend and tell him
to pass it on and nobody could stop you. A hundred prints
passed around here and there could do a lot of damage."

"We weren't ashamed of those pictures when they were
taken," Caldwell said. "We're not ashamed of them now, as
far as that goes. We're all happily married, with teen-age
children. There would be no problem explaining a thing
like that at home. I know my wife would laugh at such a
picture. But to strangers, who don't know the circumstances,
it could be quite a different matter. Scatter enough of those
pictures around and it could turn the scales against Fred."
He glanced at Babcock and then Eagan. "Tim can get a
judgeship if he wants it or he can take his chances and run for
governor, but you can bet Flynn will beat him if he possibly
can. It's not quite as bad with me, but we're an old house
and many of my most important customers are elderly people
with straight-laced ideas. I don't know how much actual business we'd lose, but I want to do what I can to be sure that
no such photographs get around."

Casey understood all of this. What he heard made sense,
but there was still one other point that bothered him.

"What makes you think Flynn actually would use those
negatives? How do you know he even wants them?"

"Keeler told us, for one," Eagan said.

"Oh?"

"Do you remember that someone tried to break into Keeler's
safe a year ago?"

"Sure," said Casey as he recalled the incident.

"The job was bungled," Eagan added. "The combination
knob was knocked off and a couple of holes were drilled, but
apparently the fellow was frightened off. The police picked
up one suspect for questioning. The clerk on the hotel desk
identified him, but there was insufficient evidence to hold him
and they had to let him go. The detectives who investigated

said he was on the payroll of Flynn Enterprises. A strong-arm type—I can't even remember his name now—who worked at the dog track Flynn controls.

"Prior to that," he said, "we heard that Flynn had been making threats of one sort or another about cutting us down to size. After that attempt on the safe we talked it over"—he glanced at his friends—"and on the assumption that Flynn might have been behind the attempt, it didn't take long for us to realize that he might have been after those old negatives. I was worried enough to go to Keeler and ask him if Flynn had ever tried to talk him out of those films, or prints of them. Keeler said yes. Flynn had been at that old party. He wasn't in any of the pictures, but he made it sound as if he wanted copies for old times' sake.

"I pointed out to Keeler then that those pictures could do us a lot of harm. I came right out and asked him for them." He took a moment to grunt softly and there was a sardonic glint in the bespectacled eyes. "At least Keeler was consistent. He said no. He said not to worry about the films. He wasn't even sure he had them, but he was going to get a new safe and he assured me that even if he had the negatives they would never be used."

"We heard he left those boxes of films to you," Babcock said, "and we made the offer to Julius Levy because it seemed the simplest thing to do. We didn't know until just now that anyone else had been bothering you about them."

"There's one thing more," Eagan said. "I take it Keeler's daughter seemed to want those films pretty badly?"

"It sounded that way," Casey said.

"Well, she's married to Stanley Garrett, isn't she? And he does promotion work for John Flynn. I suppose it could be a coincidence, but I don't like it."

"Neither do the rest of us," Caldwell said. "So that's the story and now you know why we wanted those two negatives." He came to his feet and then, as though the matter was already settled, he added: "When can we get them?"

Casey saw the others rise and he pulled himself out of the

chair. He understood their concern. He was convinced they
had told him the truth, but he was not prepared for such a
direct question and he was not even sure the films they sought
were in those two metal boxes. He said so and Eagan brushed
aside the objection.

"If they're not there, you'll still get your five thousand, so
don't worry about it," he said. "If they are there, we want
them destroyed."

The mention of the money nettled Casey because that
wasn't the reason for his hesitation. He might have explained
what he had in mind if Eagan had given him a chance, but
the district attorney was by nature an aggressive character
and he spoke impatiently.

"What's the matter?" he said. "We've told you what we
want and why. What do you want us to do, put it in writing?"

Casey tried to ignore the sarcasm.

"I'll see what I can do in the morning," he said. "I'd like
to think it over—"

"What is there to think over?" Eagan said.

"Why the morning?" Babcock pressed. "Why not right
now?"

Casey never really understood what prompted him to make
the reply he did. He was not normally a man who hedged or
resorted to subterfuge. He usually said yes or no when he
was confronted with a difficult decision; if he was right he had
the satisfaction of knowing it and if he was wrong he took
his lumps and tried to forget it.

What he should have done was tell them that he had to be
absolutely sure before he made a decision, that he wanted to
wait and see if Delemater could find the two hoodlums who
had come looking for the films, to find out who had hired
them, and be satisfied that he was doing the right thing. It
may have been because he was playing this game on a strange
field; it may have been that Eagan's sharp tongue had irritated
him. Possibly it was nothing more than a mistaken desire to
take the easy way out. Whatever the reason, he gave them a
bare-faced lie that he bitterly regretted later on.

"I haven't even got the boxes," he said. "I'll pick 'em up from Julius Levy in the morning. I'll be in touch with you then."

He saw them exchange glances. Then they were all looking at him, and he had a hard time keeping his gaze steady. He could feel the color mounting in his face and he was already ashamed of his deviousness. He wanted to swallow his pride and confess his weakness, but it was more difficult now, and as he hesitated, the moment slipped away from him and he could tell that the three men had given up on him and would plead no more.

Babcock and Eagan turned immediately to the bar wagon and pointedly fixed fresh drinks. Caldwell, still the host, was a little more polite. He made no effort to mask his disappointment and there was a brittleness to his words as he said if that was the best Casey could do they would have to accept it. He pressed a button near the doorway as he spoke, and after a few silent moments the elderly man in the dark-gray jacket appeared.

Caldwell said: "Mr. Casey is leaving, Robert." And Robert said: "This way, sir." And then Casey was in the hall being helped with his coat. The shame continued to grow in him as he rode down in the elevator, and his silent cursing did little to obviate the sense of disgust he felt for himself.

12

THERE WAS no parking ticket on Casey's windshield when he got back to his car, and he put the PRESS card back in the glove compartment. He inserted the key in the ignition switch and stepped on the starter, but he was not yet ready to drive. The feeling of shame and guilt was still with him, and there was a moment or two when he considered marching back into the apartment and confessing that he hadn't had guts enough

to give them an honest answer. Confession was said to be
good for the soul, but common sense told him that this would
be a somewhat childish display under the circumstances. He
had made a bad decision in a moment of weakness and he
was stuck with it.

He was still muttering as he drove off, and because he
did not feel like having dinner at a place where he would
have to talk to people, he chose a small and obscure restaurant that specialized in sea food. Here he was left alone
while he ate some excellent broiled scrod and a green salad.
He felt a little better when he finished and, not yet wanting
to go home, he drove to police headquarters and rode the
elevator to the fourth floor.

There was nothing he could tell Logan, but he was looking
for an antidote now and he hoped the lieutenant might
provide one if he had made any progress on the Alpert murder. But even as he walked into the squarish office, which was
sparsely furnished with a half dozen desks and chairs and a
row of filing cabinets, he could see that his luck was still bad.
There were two detectives here, one typing a report, the other
reading a newspaper. The door of the small office beyond was
open and dark, but he asked his question anyway.

"Logan out?"

"Yep," said the man with the newspaper.

"Do you know where?"

"Having his meal, I guess."

"Any idea when he'll be back?"

"Nope."

The detective at the typewriter had stopped only long
enough to make a nod of recognition, and as the clattering of
the keys continued, Casey said he would wait a few minutes.
He opened his coat and fanned it back. He sat down in a
chair near the door and reached for a cigarette. When he had
a light he sat brooding, his somber gaze moving from one
detective to the other, and up at the clock on the wall, and
back to the tips of his outstretched shoes. There were about

ten minutes of this, while the brooding got worse as the rest-lessness began to work on him.

He was not aware that he was still looking for a way out until he found one. The idea came out of nowhere and it was so simple that he took another moment to examine all its facets. The thought had as its nucleus a man named Julius Levy, and when Casey realized that through him he could save face, he asked if he could use the telephone.

Relief was already beginning to chip away at his self-induced emotional block as he reached for the directory. This, he told himself happily as he dialed the number, would do it. All he had to do was talk to Levy and tell him that he had had his conference, that he had thought the proposition over, and had decided that he was willing to play along with Babcock, Caldwell, and Eagan.

The offer had come originally from Levy; he was the inter-mediary and he could now get Casey off the hook and restore a little of his self-respect. The three men had made a case for themselves that deserved consideration and there was no reason why he shouldn't go through those films tomorrow morning and make sure the ones that worried them—if they were still in Keeler's boxes—were destroyed. He would tell Levy this and ask him to pass the word immediately to the trio.

A woman answered and when he had identified himself she said: "Oh yes, Mr. Casey. . . . I'm sorry, but Julius isn't home right now."

"Oh?" Casey said, swallowing his disappointment.

"He phoned me some time ago and said that he would get something to eat in town. He had some work to do and said he was going back to the office for a while. Perhaps you could reach him there."

Casey thanked her and said he would try it, but the instant he hung up he thought of a better way. There was no point in making a confession to the lawyer over the telephone if he could do it in person, and now he stood up and told the detective he couldn't wait for Logan any longer.

Federal Street was quiet and deserted at this hour, and Casey had no trouble finding a parking space not far from the entrance to the five-story office building. There was only one other car on that side of the street, and he paid no attention to it as he walked through the foyer to the elevator. The indicator said it was on the third floor and he brought it back, stepped in, pushed the button marked 3.

The third-floor hall stretched straight ahead of him as he stepped from the car, but there were two short transverse corridors on his immediate left and right and now, as he moved straight ahead, he thought he saw something stir in the shadows at the end of the lefthand corner. Then, before he could glance that way or even think about it, he heard the scream.

It was a startling, shocking sound, high-pitched and frightening. It had, somehow, a muffled quality, but it was a woman's scream and the sound of it left the back of Casey's neck cold and his scalp tight.

He knew it came from somewhere straight ahead and he was already running when he heard it the second time. By then he could see that a door stood open on the right side of the hall. As he realized that this was Julius Levy's office, the fear took hold of him and his nerves stretched taut and tingling.

He saw the woman as he skidded through the outer doorway. The anteroom door beside the little window stood open, and he had a clear view through the second office to the private room at the end.

She was standing just beyond the last doorway, her back to him, both hands clamped to her mouth and cheeks as though she was making a desperate effort not to scream again. She was wearing a shapeless blue work dress with an apron and he saw the pail and mop and brushes as he lunged through the second office. She had started to back away from the door when he came up behind her and turned her, hands on her shoulders to steady her, his words quick but reassuring.

"You're all right, mother," he said. "Easy now. . . . Here."

He drew her to the nearest chair and eased her into it,

pressing down on the shoulders so she would obey him, feeling her shake and speaking bluntly now because he thought it might be more effective.

"Get hold of yourself," he said. "Settle down. I may need some help."

He left her then, and as he stepped through the doorway he had the same feeling that had come to him the night he had hurried into Clem Alpert's office. Without even looking around—he had no time for that now—the impression came to him that the office had been searched. He was to remember that later, but there was no room in his mind for anything but the cold fear and foreboding as he went quickly to one knee beside the crumpled figure which was stretched near one end of the desk.

Julius Levy lay on one side, and it was this side of his head that bore the ugly wound above one ear. There was not much blood in the sparse graying hair, but the sidebow of his glasses had been broken and there was an odd look to the laceration on the skull which left Casey sick and empty inside.

He did not speak but reached for a limp wrist. He forced himself to concentrate, and as his fingers probed for a pulse beat he thought he found one. Then, knowing somehow that there was nothing he could do here to help, he came to his feet and went back to the cleaning woman. She was sitting close to a desk and he reached for the telephone and placed it in front of her.

"Feel better now?" he asked, giving her shoulder a gentle shake.

"I think so, sir."

"Good. He needs help, and quick. You're going to have to telephone, okay?" Not waiting for a reply, he dialed the number of police headquarters and made her take the telephone. "Give them the address," he ordered. "Tell them it's an emergency, that you need a doctor and an ambulance immediately."

He could tell from her reaction she was all right now, and he heard her talking as he ran back into the hall and started for the elevator. Habit was directing his movements now. The fear he had first felt had changed in character, but it was still riding him and this was his way of counteracting it. The inner sickness was there, too, but experience and training were helping him alleviate the shock of his discovery and his deep concern for the injured man.

He saw that the elevator he had so recently left—some time clock in his head told him he had been gone no more than a minute or two—was no longer here, but he did not think about it then. Neither did he want to wait, so he wheeled and pushed past a fire door and started down the steel-treaded stairs. He went through the lower lobby and past the door to the elevator with his speed unchecked, and once he reached the sidewalk, he angled toward his car. As he did so, he saw the other sedan pulling out from the curb fifty feet or so ahead of him.

He gave it no thought then because he was preoccupied with other things, but as he unlocked the rear deck of his car and reached for his camera, he had the impression that the car was a foreign make and he noticed the license number, not because he thought it made any difference but because its four-digit number set it apart from the majority of others.

The cleaning woman was still in the chair, her hand on the telephone, when he came back to the center office. There was recognition in her glance as he went past her, and more color in her face, and he knew that she would be all right. He said nothing at all as he took his two pictures, and he came back to her just as two uniformed officers from the squad car strode into the anteroom.

After that, Casey sat in the middle office and waited, a burly, disconsolate figure, his unseeing gaze darkly troubled and a new feeling of guilt working insidiously inside him. He kept his camera beside him because he had plenty of time to get the films back to the office. He answered the original questions and repeated those answers to the detectives from the precinct house who followed the men from the squad car. He spoke when spoken to, but he made no advance of his own until Levy had been carried away on a stretcher and the doctor appeared from the inner office.

"What are his chances?" he asked, pushing out of the chair and intercepting the man.

"Not good."

"But he's got a chance, hasn't he?"

"I'd rather not say. His pulse is weak and I don't like the lack of reaction in his pupils."

"What happens now?"

"A neuro-surgeon is on his way to the hospital. What happens now is up to him."

Casey sat down again. He paid no attention to the traffic that went in and out of the office, and the comments he heard from time to time did not register. He heard the repeated questions directed to the cleaning woman and was aware that some considerate detective told her she had better call it a night and arranged to have her driven home. He was still sitting there when someone stopped in front of him. When the figure did not move, he glanced up and found Lieutenant Logan watching him.

The sight of the lieutenant brought a greater disturbance to his thoughts. "How come?" he demanded, an edge in his voice because of the inner pressure. "This isn't homicide."

"I got the word it could be," Logan said. "I thought I might as well get some of the details firsthand."

"I stopped at your place," Casey said.

"They told me." Logan tugged at his hat brim. "What did you want to see me about?"

"Nothing in particular," Casey said, knowing this was the truth. "I just wanted to see if you'd made any progress on the Alpert thing."

"Not much." Logan pulled a straight-backed chair close and straddled it, his elbows on the top, as he continued to inspect the big photographer. "You got to Alpert's place because you spotted a squad car that was in a hurry. What brought you here?"

Casey thought it over and was further depressed. How, he

asked himself, could he tell Logan about the film boxes now, after he had talked with the three men at Caldwell's apartment? What could he say without violating a confidence?

"I just wanted to talk to him," he said without any great conviction. "Levy was Keeler's executor and I had the job of disposing of his cameras and equipment for the estate."

"But why tonight?"

"No reason," Casey said defensively. "I called Levy's home and his wife said he was working. I didn't have anything else to do so I thought I'd drop by and tell him what I'd been doing. . . . Do you think someone searched the place?" he asked, wanting to change the subject. "Like at Alpert's?"

"Could be," Logan said. "That steel filing cabinet was busted open. The way it looks now, Levy walked in on the guy and got slugged before he knew what it was all about."

"Haven't you got anything?"

"We've got some fingerprints, but they'll probably turn out to belong to the help. We're checking the secretary and that young fellow who worked for him to see what appointments he had today and if anyone came to see him this afternoon. We could use a little help. I mean," he added with just a faint note of sarcasm, "if you just happen to remember something."

The tone was not lost on Casey, and it had the effect of making him concentrate for the first time. He remembered the car that had pulled away from him when he had run out to get his camera. He spoke of it now. He answered questions about the position of the elevator as Logan explored the possibility. He said the car probably didn't mean anything, but Logan could check it if he wanted to.

When he finished, the lieutenant went into the inner office and spoke to one of the detectives. Casey could hear him on the telephone, and he got enough of the conversation to understand that he was talking to someone in the Department of Motor Vehicles.

The detective got good service, and when Logan came back three minutes later he said: "If you had the license right, it was issued to a Donald Caldwell. Isn't he the broker? Caldwell and Jennings?"

Casey said yes; then, even as his thoughts sought some channel of understanding, the lie he had told two hours earlier suddenly came back to haunt him. He tried to evade the implication and could not, and the sickness that had been up to now under some control attacked him fully. He tried to tell himself that Caldwell could not be responsible for what had happened to Julius Levy. He recalled again the two hoodlums who had come to his place last night. By now they must know the truth about the films they had taken. At the time he had told them Levy had the films they wanted, which was true, and he clung to the thought that they had come here earlier to try again.

This was a supposition he could accept, but it was not the only one. Caldwell, Babcock, and Eagan had been told that Levy still had the negative boxes. They had no reason to doubt that statement. As he struggled with the new sense of guilt that threatened to overwhelm him, he could believe that the three men, acting in concert, could not have done this thing. But individual initiative and action was something else again.

Any one of them, realizing the risk but driven by some unmanageable fear of exposure, could have taken a chance and come here to get those boxes. For this was not a premeditated attack. All signs indicated that whoever had struck Levy down had been surprised in his work and had slugged the lawyer to protect his identity. Many men might react in a similar fashion if panic proved stronger than reason, even high-placed and successful men like Caldwell, Babcock, and Eagan.

The shrill ringing of the telephone checked these thoughts and brought a momentary relief from his self-recriminations, and he listened while the detective in the private office replied. When he had asked two or three questions which meant nothing to Casey, he called to Logan.

"Maybe you ought to take this, Lieutenant."

Logan rose and moved inside, closing the door behind him.

Casey sat where he was and sweated it out until the lieutenant came back. This time he leaned against the edge of the desk and his lean, angular face held a new tightness and his eyes were full of thought.

"Were you very close to Levy?" he asked quietly.

"Not close. I liked him."

"That was the hospital. It's homicide now. He died on the table before they could operate. The doctor says some people have thinner skulls than others. Levy was one of them."

He paused, looking down at Casey and seeing his distress. He did not try to understand why the big photographer was so moved, but his voice was sympathetic when he spoke.

"I guess you got your pictures when you came."

"I got them." Casey got to his feet with an effort and reached for his camera. He was deliberate when he straightened his hat. He took a long audible breath and brought his shoulders back. "I guess I better get them back to the office."

"Do that," Logan said. "There's nothing for you here. If you think of anything, try me in the morning."

Casey said he would and started for the anteroom, his gait slow, deliberate, and heavy.

13

THE APARTMENT HOUSE that Johnny Keeler held title to had a conservative, settled look; its dark-red façade had a well-kept appearance; and the foyer was clean and well-lighted when Casey walked in at ten o'clock on his way home from the *Express*. The elevator was unoccupied and he did not have to wait long after he had pushed the buzzer at apartment 3-D.

Alma Jensen opened her green eyes the moment she saw him standing there, and the look that followed seemed both cordial and pleasantly surprised. When she stepped back to let him enter, he saw she was clad in flannel slacks and a cashmere pullover that did nice things for her big-boned but shapely body. She was tall enough to be able to wear the outfit with a grace many women might have envied, and Casey was reminded again that this was a very attractive female.

"Why Jack," she said. "How nice. Come in, come in."

"You said to stop by," Casey said as he took off his hat.

"And I meant it. Here, let me have your coat, too."

He said he could take it and folded it across the back of a nearby chair. He said he wouldn't stay long and she said she was about to have a nightcap and what would he like?

"Johnny preferred bourbon," she said, "but I think there may be some Scotch, too."

"Bourbon would be fine," Casey said. "Can I help?"

"I've had a lot of practice," she said, "and I know where everything is. . . . Sit over here. I won't be a minute."

Casey watched her disappear beyond a swinging door and moved over to the chair she had indicated. The room had a feminine quality in its pastel colors, but the furnishings were comfortable-looking and conservative. The divan was roomy, the chairs good-sized, and there were plenty of lamps. The big wingchair she had indicated had a magazine rack on one side and an end table on the other, and it was so situated that it afforded a good view of the television set. A floor lamp gave it plenty of light, and he wondered if this was where Keeler used to sit. He asked about it when she came back with the drinks.

"Yes," she said. "Sometimes, like on a Sunday, he would hardly get out of it all day long."

Casey accepted the man-sized highball, and the color told him that she had not been stingy with the whisky. He watched her go over to the divan and settle in one corner, her legs drawn up sideways, with the knees sharply bent.

"He liked it here," she said, and there was a small and wistful smile in the green eyes as she spoke. "He didn't come as often as he might have, but when he did, he could relax."

"I'm sure he could," Casey said.

"Johnny was a lonely man these past years," she added as though she had not heard. "He worked too hard but he liked doing it, and he was usually tired out when he came. I'm a fairly good cook, and I like to cook, and that made it easy. He didn't want me to go to the Avon, but he could count on my being here when he needed me. He'd look at television a while, and read some, and we'd play gin rummy when he got bored. He'd tell me his troubles, and we would do a little quiet drinking."

She took a sip of her highball and said: "But it wasn't all one-sided. I don't want you to think that. A woman who has been married and reasonably happy with that marriage gets lonely, too. Maybe it isn't important when you're young, but when you get to be forty—" She hesitated and moistened her lips. "I think I would have married Johnny if he had asked, but he thought he was too old to try again. He always remembered that the first time had been a failure and I guess he didn't want to take another chance."

She said other things, but Casey did not hear them. His mind was too full of brooding to pay close attention, but he was not aware of this until she spoke to him directly.

"I'm sorry," he said. "I guess I was thinking about something else."

"I know you were," she said. "You're worried. Something's bothering you. Is it about Johnny?" she added on a note of quick concern.

He shook his head and then, because he knew there would be questions he wanted to ask, he told her about Julius Levy. He heard her say. "Oh, how awful!" but he went on, giving some of his thoughts about the two boxes of films which may have been responsible for the lawyer's death, not mentioning names but giving her the general picture.

"I can't help thinking," he said when he finished, "that there must be some connection between what happened to Levy and what happened to Clem Alpert." He leaned forward slightly, watching her now as he added: "There's no question

about Johnny, is there? I mean, about his dying from a stroke
or a hemorrhage?"

"None." She met his gaze with steady eyes. "Why do you
ask?"

"I don't know," Casey said. "I guess I don't know anything
any more. But I keep thinking of Johnny and Alpert. I keep
wondering what Alpert was doing there Saturday night. I
wish you'd tell me again exactly what you did when you came
into the room that night. You said Johnny was stretched out
on the floor. Was Alpert actually trying to lift him?"

"Why—I thought he was. He was on one knee beside Johnny
and his back was turned. I didn't know what had happened
and I guess I was pretty badly frightened. I asked Alpert what
was the matter and he said he didn't know."

"You helped Alpert lift Johnny to the couch. Then what? I
mean, what did you do?"

He heard her trying to answer his question, but what she
said was not much help and he could understand why. She
had been scared and she hadn't known what happened or
what was wrong with Keeler. She had stayed there by the
couch on her knees for a while, talking to him and trying to
rouse him. She did not know what Alpert had been doing during that time, but she knew he had not yet called for a doctor
because she asked him.

"I was the one who called the doctor," she said.

"You don't know what Alpert was doing while you were on
the telephone, do you?"

"No. I wasn't thinking about him then. Why? What's so
important about what *he* was doing?"

Casey took another swallow of his drink. He was still leaning forward in his chair, the glass in both hands, and when
he had studied it a moment he realized that if he expected any
help he would have to do a little confiding of his own. With
this in mind, he told her of his suspicions of Alpert and his
theory about the negatives the detective might have taken
from Keeler's safe. He said it was probable that there had
been enough time for Alpert to take the keys from Keeler's

pocket and remove anything he wanted from that safe. He expanded on the theory as he explained the circumstances of Alpert's death. He told her that the office had been thoroughly searched and that the killer might well have been after negatives that Alpert had taken. He said that Julius Levy's office had also been searched.

"Apparently he walked in on this guy, whoever he was, and got slugged too hard."

The frown had been working deeper above the green eyes as the woman listened, and even when Casey finished it was apparent that she did not know what he was driving at. She said so.

"But I still don't understand."

"Understand what?"

"The way you've been talking, anyone would think you were responsible," she said. "Suppose your theory is right. Suppose there is some connection between what happened to Alpert and to Mr. Levy. I still don't see—"

"Maybe I am responsible," Casey said.

He took a small breath and then, because he could no longer contain all these things that were bottled up inside him, he began to speak of details that he had heretofore kept to himself. It may have been his feeling of guilt and responsibility; it may have been just a simple need to talk and get certain things in the open so they could better be explained. Whatever the reason, he told her about the two hoodlums who had come to his apartment with a gun; he told her of the offer Julius Levy had made. Without mentioning any names, he spoke of the three men who had made that offer and drew a rough verbal picture of why certain negatives were important. He told her he had lied about the whereabouts of those boxes, and he confessed that he lacked the guts to go back to them and admit the truth.

"Oh," she said when he finished. "And you think that one of these men might have gone to Mr. Levy's office to look for those boxes?"

"It could have happened that way."

"Then where are they now?"

Casey told her that, too. He explained where he had put the two boxes and tried to tell her why.

"There's one other thing," he said. "Sheila Garrett came to the office this afternoon and made a pitch for those negatives." He tried to quote from the dialogue, and when he was through, he said: "You know how it was between Keeler and his daughter. Do you think she was leveling with me? Do you think it was really sentiment that—"

"No," she said, interrupting. She gave a small but deliberate shake of her head, and Casey saw the reddish glints in the soft darkness of her hair. "Not for a minute," she said emphatically. "She tried that once before, last year."

"Tried what once before?"

"To get those boxes of films. I don't mean to keep. Just to look at, or so she said. Johnny told me she came to see him with some story about wanting to see what kind of pictures he'd been saving so long. She had never shown any interest in what he did—this was what she told him—and she felt a little guilty about it. She thought it would be nice if she could understand and appreciate his work a little better. If she could have them for a few days, she could go through them, like a family album; she thought it might be fun.

"Johnny didn't understand her, but he didn't believe the story, not for a minute. She had never paid the slightest bit of attention to his work. All this new interest surprised him at first, and he questioned her, and the answers she gave him made him suspicious. He tried to be nice about it and explain why he never let anyone see his old films, and when he continued to question her she got annoyed and flounced off."

Casey kept thinking as the story unfolded. He found himself wondering if this first request of Sheila Garrett's had any connection with the attempt that had been made to break into Keeler's safe.

"I didn't know that," he said, "but I'm just as glad I didn't fall for her story."

"So am I. I've no idea what she wanted with those boxes,

but from what I've seen of her, she's a very selfish woman and if she had any great feeling of sentiment for Johnny over the years she never made any honest attempt to show it."

She stopped abruptly, her expression softening as though she realized how what she had said sounded.

"Perhaps I shouldn't be so positive," she said. "Naturally I'm prejudiced. She knew about Johnny and me; he made no bones about it. I don't suppose she could be blamed for resenting me. I might have felt the same way if the circumstances were reversed, but she seemed to forget that Johnny was sixty years old and had a right to do what he wanted to. She didn't stop to wonder if this relationship might be good for him or consider the possibility that it might be giving him a little happiness. What she was afraid of was that he might marry me and leave the bulk of his estate to me instead of to her." She hesitated again and uttered a small sigh. "I guess this must sound pretty bitchy to you, but I think it's the truth; I honestly do."

Casey had been listening with part of his mind while the other reached for more answers.

"Would Sheila have asked for those two boxes because her husband told her to?"

"Yes, I think she would."

"Stan Garrett knew those films had been left to me as soon as he heard the will. He works for Big John Flynn and I happen to know Flynn would like to get one or two of those negatives. Flynn or Garrett could have hired those two hoods."

"Couldn't they also have gone to Mr. Levy's office tonight?"

"I suppose they could have," Casey said and then, his mind moving off on a tangent, he thought: *Why don't I hear from Sam Delemater? Why doesn't he turn up those two hoods?*

The thought, which had come out of nowhere, had a therapeutic effect on his mental depression and brought with it a sudden impatience. To give it an outlet, he glanced up and asked if he could use the telephone.

There was a directory in the cabinet underneath the little table, and he tried Delemater's home address first. Counting the rings until he was sure there would be no answer, he hung up and tried the office number. There was no answer here either, but since there was still another alternative, he dialed the number of the *Express* and asked for the studio. This time his luck was in and he got the answer he wanted.

"Yeah," Lanvin said. "He called about five minutes ago. They've been trying to get your car on the radio."

"Okay. What's the message?"

Lanvin gave him a telephone number and an extension. He repeated it aloud, broke the connection, and dialed again.This time the answer came almost immediately and the voice was instantly familiar.

"I finally got something for you," Delemater said.

"What?"

"Never mind what. Just get down here on the double," Delemater said and gave Casey an address. "How long will you be?"

"Ten minutes at the outside."

Casey hung up and there was a gleam in the dark eyes where none had been before. The news had started a small tingle of excitement deep inside him, and he quickly tossed off his drink and put the glass aside. Alma Jensen, who had come to her feet, asked if it was good news and he said he hoped so. She helped him on with his coat and then he turned, standing close as he faced her.

"The other night when I drove you home you said you didn't know why Johnny and Clem Alpert were together Saturday night. Is that the truth?"

"If you mean literally, yes it was the truth."

"But you could maybe guess why."

"Maybe, but I'm not going to. I think it's too late for guessing."

She was looking right at him as she spoke, a calmness in her face and the green eyes steady. Something about her words told him that she meant what she said, but he had to try once more.

"It could be important, Alma."

She reached up and took hold of his lapels, gently pulling them together and adding a small pat to make sure they were smooth. She gave him a small smile, and there was a hint of sadness in it as she continued to inspect him.

"Not to Johnny," she said. "I have to think of him, don't I?"

Casey couldn't argue with that. He squeezed her hand and stepped back. He thanked her for the drink and said he'd see her, and she said to make it soon.

14

THE BAKER HOTEL was a six-story brick structure with discolored walls and a depressing outlook. Decay had set in many years ago, and although the location remained reasonably central, the railroad cut-out which ran almost directly in front of it made it a problem for light sleepers. Such innovations as air conditioning and television had not yet been installed, but the rates were modest and the management had trained the desk clerks to require a minimum of information about its guests. Rent in advance was sometimes required from questionable tenants, but the guests who were attracted here were not the sort to complain of minor inconveniences.

Casey had been here before, but not recently, and he was accorded no more than a glance from the desk clerk. The seedy-looking house detective, who had an elbow planted on the counter, eyed him sleepily as he turned toward the elevators, but the ancient operator had no comment to make as they rode to the fourth floor. Casey was looking for room 414, and when he found it near the end of a corridor, he hesitated a second and crossed his fingers mentally before he knocked.

The voice that responded said: "It's open," and Casey walked into a sizable, high-ceilinged room to find Sam Delemater and the redheaded gunman he had seen before facing him. Delemater, his coat still on and his hat pushed back, looked completely at ease, but a change had been made in the redhead's face.

He was sitting in a corner in a narrow straight-backed chair, its odd position suggesting that it had been placed there deliberately. He was in his shirt sleeves, and the thin, pale face still looked mean, but with a difference. It was a cowed, sullen, and subdued meanness, and the bony features were embellished with a sizable bruise under one eye that was already turning blue and a noticeable puffiness at one side of the mouth.

The sight of Delemater sitting quietly next to the youth, the look of complete unconcern on the round, familiar face, brought a grin to Casey's eyes, and for the first time that day he had the warm and comforting feeling that things were starting to go his way at last.

"What did you do to him?" he said as he closed the door and leaned up against it.

"Nothing." Delemater lifted a short-barreled revolver Casey had not seen before. "He tried to use this on me and I took it away from him."

This, if one knew Delemater well, was wholly understandable. He did not look formidable and his stocky build was not impressive, but he had learned his self-defense lessons well at the police academy years ago and he was not yet too old to practice them when necessary.

"His name is Harold Vernon," he said now. "That's all I've got so far. I decided to wait for you."

"How'd you find him?"

"I got a lead from a guy. Funny thing about that, too. The lead was to his pal. Name of Ostrowski. Came up here to have a look and ran right into junior."

Casey glanced about the room, which, except for its size, was in character with the hotel itself. Its air of mediocrity had been stamped upon the twin beds, the chest, the bureau, the chairs, and the inadequate lighting. A suitcase stood next to one of the beds, and newspapers, magazines, and used towels completed the picture of untidiness.

"I think junior's from out of town," Delemater added. "Shall we find out?"

"Let's," Casey said as he advanced.

"Lay off," the redhead said in whispered tones. "If you think you've got anything on me, call a cop."

"Later," said Delemater. "Let's see your wallet."

The reply was obscene, but Delemater took no notice of it. He just reached out and belted the other across the mouth with the palm of his hand with sufficient force to rock the youth's head and send the straight hair on end. When Vernon started to jump up, Delemater pushed him back. He lifted his hand again, still not saying a word, and this time the youth ducked and reached for the wallet in his hip pocket.

"What did you do with my box of films?" Casey said as Delemater inspected the wallet.

"They're where we said they'd be. In a South Station locker."

"Where's the key?"

"Frank's got it."

"Frank who?"

"Frank Ostrowski."

"Junior's from Jersey City," Delemater said and held up some bills he had taken from the inner compartment. "And pretty well heeled. Four hundred bucks in new fifties."

"Is that what you got for crashing my place the other night?" Casey asked. "Who hired you?"

Vernon glared at him but said nothing, and in that moment of silence Casey's ear caught a faint sound of movement in the hall. Listening now, with his senses suddenly alert and groping, he thought he could make out muffled steps approaching. When they stopped outside the door, he wheeled and started for it. In that same instant a key scratched in the lock and Casey signaled in pantomime to Delemater, jabbing his finger in Vernon's direction.

Delemater got the message. He came out of his chair and stood close to the youth, one hand clamped across his mouth to prevent his giving any word of warning.

Casey was behind the door as it opened. He saw the man in the dark coat and narrow-brimmed hat take one step forward and stop as he spotted Delemater and Vernon across the room. He seemed to stiffen for an instant as he swung the door behind him; then he thrust his hand into his coat pocket.

Casey only had to take one step. The fellow saw him as he moved, but by that time it was too late.

He jerked the hand out and Casey, not knowing what would be in it, chopped at the wrist with the side of his left hand. The blow would have done credit to a Karate expert, and as the blackjack spun across the room, Casey let go with his right.

It was a made-to-order situation now and no great skill was required. He had the advantage of surprise and position. He was close enough for a hook and he put his thighs and shoulder behind the blow, leaning into it with enthusiasm. He felt the welcome shock in his forearm as his fist crashed solidly into the side of the fellow's jaw, and that was that.

Ostrowski went down so hard the walls shook, his hat tumbling to one side as he fell. He hit the floor in a sitting position, more shaken than hurt, and after a second or two his eyes cleared and he blinked and shook his head. When he started to rise Casey helped him. He grabbed hold of the front of the coat and lifted, turning the man toward a chair near the window.

Ostrowski made one more try, but it was a mistake. The broad face had a red mark at the side of the jaw and the eyes beneath the scarred brows were furious. He was too close to use his hands, but he tried to use his knee, and Casey diagnosed the move and got his hip in the way. Then, letting go of the front of the coat, he pushed with one hand and added further impetus with a backhand swipe across the opposite cheek.

Ostrowski went into the chair hard, and his body kept right on going as it tipped over backward. He hit the floor on the back of his neck and rolled over. He got up slowly, warily, his face full of doubt and indecision. He glanced at Casey, who made no attempt to follow him. He looked over at his companion, and Delemater, who had removed his hand from the redhead's mouth, showed him the gun.

Nothing was said while Ostrowski picked up the chair and straightened his coat. He walked over and retrieved his hat. He punched the crown back into shape and put it on. He began to massage the back of his thick neck, and when Casey told him to sit down, he did so.

"Where's the key?"

"What key?"

"The key to that South Station locker."

Ostrowski reached into his pocket and produced it. "We were going to send it to you anyway."

Casey glanced at the number on it, slipped it into his pocket. He went over and picked up the blackjack. He had not the slightest intention of using it, but Ostrowski didn't know that and his eyes were again wary as Casey advanced. When Casey asked for his wallet, he hesitated only momentarily before reaching into an inside pocket and producing it.

Casey verified the name Delemater had given him. It was on the driver's license and a social security card. In the bill compartment he found a twenty, a ten, and a check that helped to make the evening worthwhile.

It was made out to Frank Ostrowski in the amount of one hundred and fifty dollars. It was signed by an unfamiliar name over the title of cashier, and the imprint at the top said *Flynn Enterprises.*

"Is it pay day, Frank?"

Ostrowski said nothing, and Casey walked over to show the check to Delemater. The wastebasket stood nearby and he dropped the blackjack into it. He put the check back into the wallet and returned it.

"A hundred and fifty bucks," he said. "Is that what you got for stealing my films? Who hired Vernon, you or Flynn?"

Ostrowski folded his arms and sat mute.

"What're you afraid of?" Casey said.

"I work for the company," Ostrowski said. "That's a company check."

"But John Flynn hired you."

"Hah! Big John don't even speak to me."

Casey started to pursue the subject; then, aware that Ostrowski had spoken with a certain conviction, he stopped as a new thought came to him. If the story Caldwell, Babcock, and Eagan had told him was true—and he had no reason to doubt it—John Flynn wanted certain negatives. But that did not mean that Flynn himself had hired either Ostrowski or the redhead. Flynn was the top man, but his position was such that he would be unlikely to deal directly with hired muscle. But there was another man in the organization who seemed now to fit very neatly into the picture.

Stanley Garrett worked for Flynn. Garrett had heard Keeler's will and knew that the boxes of films had been left to Casey. He and his wife had left Levy's office before Casey, and it would be logical for Garrett to assume that Casey had taken the films that first morning. If Garrett had passed the word to Flynn—

Casey left the thought unfinished because, in the light of other things he had learned, he no longer needed it.

"Okay, Frankie," he said. "Flynn didn't hire you. My friend and I"—he glanced at Delemater—"don't want to work you over if we don't have to. Just give me the initials of the guy who did hire you. Don't get cute either, because I know a lot more about this than I did. Give me the right initials and we'll take a walk."

Ostrowski took a breath. He glanced at Vernon and back at Casey. He gave a small shake of his head that had no particular significance and by that time he had made up his mind.

"S. G."

"Okay." Casey let his breath out slowly and felt his muscles start to relax. He glanced over at Delemater and grinned. "Let's go, Sam."

Delemater stood up and moved away from Vernon. "What

do you want to do with them?" he asked. "Take them down to the precinct?"

"For what?" Casey said. "So Flynn's lawyers can spring them?"

"Yeah, I guess you're right." Delemater glanced first at one man and then at the other; finally he, too, grinned. "After what happened here, they might even file counter-complaints, hunh?"

He moved over to join Casey, and Vernon, relieved of the pressure of the detective's presence, came to his feet.

"What about my gun?"

Delemater held it up and examined it anew. He flipped the cylinder out and dumped the shells into his hand. He jiggled them in his palm for a second or two and then tossed them on the bed.

"I'll leave you the slugs, Junior. I'll just add this to my collection."

"Now wait," Vernon said, bristling.

Delemater cut him off. "When I went through your wallet I didn't see any permit to carry a gun. You could get arrested."

There was no further protest from either man as they left the room, and when they came out on the street and stood a moment on the sidewalk, Delemater said: "You owe me forty-five bucks, plus ten for the guy who tipped me."

"Okay," Casey said. "How's my credit?"

"Good. Why?"

"You're not through. I want one more day's work. Do you know a blonde named Fay Novak? She used to be married to Clem Alpert."

"I know who she is. She did a little work for Alpert now and then."

"What kind of work?"

"Well, you know. There're times in this racket when you can use a woman. They can be very helpful, especially in domestic squabbles. But why do you need me? You should be able to find out where she lives."

"Sure," Casey said. "But I don't think she's staying there now." He went on to tell Delemater what he had in mind and explained how he had put the girl in the cab the night before. "It's a Red-and-White," he said, "and the driver's name is Rudy Kowalchik."

He told the detective where he had stopped the taxi and gave him an approximate time.

"Get on it the first thing in the morning, will you, Sam? You can get to Kowalchik through the dispatcher, and when you find out where he dropped her, start working. Call me when you locate her."

"You make it sound easy," Delemater said.

"For forty-five bucks a day it should be easy?"

"Okay," Delemater said and chuckled. "I'll get on it. Where you going now?"

"I'm going down to the South Station and get my films and then I'm going home," Casey said. "It's been one hell of a long day."

15

WHEN Sam Delemater came out of his apartment at nine o'clock the next morning, the sun was out and the breeze which had been bringing the damp chill in from the ocean had shifted to the southwest. He took a couple of sample breaths of the clear bright air and when he found it pleasing to his lungs he started briskly down the street toward the Hotel Alpert, which stood a block and a half away. This was always his first stop of the day because the newsstand girl saved the necessary racing papers for him. Usually he took them into breakfast with him, but this morning he moved directly from the newsstand to the telephone booth, where he dialed the number of the Red-and-White Cab Company.

He knew the dispatcher slightly, and it was a simple matter

to explain what he had in mind. The fact that the Red-and-White cabs were radio-controlled was a help now, and he kept the wire open until the dispatcher came back with the word that Rudy Kowalchik had just then parked his cab in the stand at the corner of Boylston and Park.

"Good," Delemater said. "Tell him to start the meter—on me —and wait."

The garage where he kept his car was just around the corner. He started there now, deciding that breakfast could wait a while, for, despite the fact that he gave perhaps too much time to the horses, he was a conscientious man when he was being paid to work, and for someone like Casey he wanted to give full value for the money received.

A five-minute drive took him to the proper corner. Rudy Kowalchik's cab was the second in line, and he eased his sedan up close and double-parked while he slid over on the seat and lowered the window.

"Kowalchik?"

"Right."

"What have you got on the meter?"

"Seventy cents."

Delemater found two dollar bills and held them out the window. "I'm doing a little job for Jack Casey," he said. "He says he put a blonde in your cab night before last."

"Yeah," said Kowalchik, reaching for the two dollars.

"Casey's looking for her," Delemater said. "Where did you drop her?"

"At the corner of Davis and Spring."

Delemater took a moment to visualize the location and then said: "Davis is a dead-end street, isn't it?"

"That's right. It's only a block long."

"Which way did she walk?"

"Down Davis," Kowalchik said, "and if it's any help to you, she started down the right side. She could have crossed over— I didn't watch her long—but that's the side she started on."

It was only a six- or seven-minute drive to the corner Kowalchik had mentioned, and Delemater stopped his car opposite Davis Street to do a little reconnoitering. This did not take long and what he saw was encouraging in more ways than one.

Some peculiarity of city planning, either on the part of the founding fathers or of some later group, had decreed that Davis Street should be only one block long. What had terminated it originally Delemater did not know, but now it ended in a blank brick wall which was part of a warehouse facing the other way. On the left side was a row of ancient brownstones; on the right were more brownstones and two modest, three-story beige-brick apartments, apparently walk-ups. Spring Street, opposite the entrance to Davis, had a somewhat more prosperous look. Here the apartments were larger and more pretentious, but at the moment it was the two opposite corners that interested Delemater most.

On his left was a small drugstore and next to it a tiny neighborhood newsstore and tobacco shop. Opposite this was a café or tavern that looked as if it might serve breakfast. What he needed first was a parking place, and it came to him now how much easier things would be if he could operate like the private dicks in television. In such shows parking was never a problem. Always the young, handsome, and intrepid operators pulled their shiny convertibles into a space exactly where they needed one. Day or night, the city streets they prowled were sufficiently empty for their purpose. If they needed an opening in front of an office building, bank, or night club, it was there. If they were waiting to tail a suspect, there was a perfect spot directly across the street or down the block where they could sit unobserved with the top of the convertible down. . . .

He chuckled to himself as his mind envisioned such a utopia, for at the moment he was double-parked on Spring and wondering what to do next, and he thought: *Cut it out, Sam. If you're going to be jealous of these TV characters, stick to essentials. Instead of envying them their parking places, why not ask for some of those young blonde numbers they always have as clients?*

The daydream left a broad grin on his face, but he had been thinking with the practical part of his mind as the traffic rolled past, and by then he had a solution to his problem, which, even in real life, presented no great difficulties.

He needed a place to park, and he finally saw one that would serve his purpose. Because he could not foresee what might happen, he wanted to be ready to move. For this reason he cramped the wheel and turned down Davis, made a U-turn at the end, and came back to an empty spot just short of the tobacco store.

There was, he knew, a possibility that some casual inquiries at the tavern and drugstore and tobacco shop might give him a lead on Fay Novak. She was reasonably attractive and had a neat figure; the tinted blonde hair should help make her more noticeable than the average neighborhood housewife. Someone might remember her, but he would need plenty of luck to get a lead on where she was staying and he knew he could not count on that. He had to find a way to get the doors of each apartment open, and he now recalled a method he had used before.

To put himself in business, all he needed was a newspaper, and since Casey was paying him he would buy a copy of the *Express*. With this under his arm and a notebook and pencil in his hand, he would become Sam Delemater, a subscription salesman for the *Morning Express*. He would take no subscriptions, but he would find out who subscribed to the *Express* and get comments on what the readers liked and did not like. The nonsubscribers needed a different approach, but since all he wanted was to get doors to open and to find out who occupied the various apartments, the questions he would ask were unimportant.

Now, getting out of his car, he was reminded again that he had had no breakfast, and then, as he considered the newsstore and the tavern, a surprising and welcome thought struck him. As it began to blossom, he considered its possibilities; he pursued it still more and was encouraged.

The basic factor in the idea was the character of the woman

he sought. From what Casey had said, Fay Novak had left her own apartment to stay with a friend. Why was no concern of his. She had apparently taken no clothes with her. She had said she was going to stay with a girl-friend. She was a city-bred girl who had worked in night clubs and bars and cocktail lounges. He had known other women like her and he had learned that a daily newspaper, particularly in the morning, was a necessary part of their existence.

The more he considered the idea the better he liked it. He knew he could always do the leg work if the hunch didn't pay off, and with this in mind, he stepped into the shop and picked up a copy of the *Express* and a pack of cigarettes. The stooped and elderly proprietor had no other customer at the moment so he asked about Fay Novak, describing her with an accuracy that he had learned long ago.

"She probably came in yesterday morning," he said. "Maybe she's already been here today."

"Not today," the proprietor said. "But there was a girl in yesterday that sounds like the one you mean. Stranger in the neighborhood. Yellow hair like you said, plenty of perfume. Bought papers and cigarettes and gum."

Delemater thanked him and crossed over to the tavern. He said good morning to the husky man who was working behind the bar and asked if he could get some breakfast.

"Maybe some tomato juice," he said when the man said yes. "With a couple of fried eggs, toast, and coffee."

"Sure. How do you like the eggs?"

"Over easy," Delemater said and turned to inspect the interior.

Two men in working clothes occupied bar stools at the far end, and a woman with her hair in curlers and a bandana sat at a table sipping coffee and smoking a cigarette. There was a row of booths along one wall and some tables near the front, and Delemater picked one next to the window overlooking Davis Street and the corner. He glanced at the front page of the *Express* while the barman set a place for him and brought him his juice. He asked if he could adjust the Vene-

tian blinds so he could see better, and when he had finished his
view was unobstructed.

He read about Julius Levy while he drank his juice, and he
was just getting to work on his eggs when Fay Novak walked
past the window and started across the street at the corner.
When she stepped into the tobacco shop, he began to eat as
fast as he could, not wanting to leave the rest of his breakfast
but knowing he had to follow her when she left.

But in this assumption he was happily wrong. When the
girl reappeared she crossed the street, walked past the window as Delemater was getting to his feet, and turned into the
doorway. There was just time enough for him to get back into
the chair and lift the paper when she walked behind him.
She was so close he could smell her, and he got one more
break when she headed for the bar and ordered coffee. This
gave him time to move the chair so his back was turned
diagonally, and then, not waiting for the coffee, she continued on to the telephone booth at the rear.

It was when she came back to the bar stool and lit a cigarette that he got the idea she might be waiting for someone.
When she asked for a second cup of coffee he was sure of it,
and now, satisfied that she would be here a while, he turned
to his racing papers and began to figure out how he had done
the day before. There was a pattern to what he did, for this
was part of his daily routine and came under the head of
economics and research. His notebook gave him a record of all
bets he had made at various tracks, and he added to his figures
as he jotted down official results. Basic mathematics took
over from there and when the figures were in he saw that he
had bet a total of one hundred and eighty dollars all told, from
which there was a net profit on the day of a dollar and seventy
cents.

Well, kid, he thought as he put his notebook away, *at least
you were in the black on the day and if that damned Skyhigh
hadn't been practically left at the post at Gulfstream, you
would have won big. Oh, well, today's another day.*

He was doing his preliminary groundwork for the afternoon

when the door opened and a man passed behind him. From
the corner of his eye he saw the blonde slip from the stool.
Because he was afraid to turn round, he sat where he was,
hearing the low words of greeting. He could not translate
them, but he heard the girl say: "No, I paid for the coffee," and
then they were moving toward the door together.

As soon as they left, Delemater picked up his papers and
put a dollar bill on the table. Since no one passed the window, he knew the couple must have turned the other way and
now he went outside, saw that he was right, and crossed to
the opposite side of the street. From here he could easily see
which building they entered, but it did not happen quite that
way.

They stopped in front of the first of the two modest apartments, and he realized that the man was tall and bulky. He
held the blonde's arm possessively with one hand and walked
as far as the entrance. Even from where he stood, Delemater
could see him nod and tip his hat politely; then, as the girl
disappeared, the man started briskly back down the street,
jaywalking across the empty pavement as he approached.

Delemater had reached the age where few things in his
line of work surprised him, and he stepped past the glass
door of the drugstore to consider the situation. He had about
ten seconds to make up his mind, but it did not take him that
long to reach a decision. Casey had given him the job of locat-
ing Fay Novak. He had already done so. He could now telephone Casey and wait for further instructions about the
girl, or he could follow the man and perhaps give Casey an unexpected bonus.

He watched him move past the front of the drugstore, and
there was something so intent and purposeful about the way
he walked that Delemater decided to stick with him a while
longer. His own car was so parked that he could reach it
quickly if the man started looking for a taxi. With this in
mind, he eased out of the drugstore as the man turned right.
When he cautiously made the same turn, he saw the fellow

plugging steadily along with no backward glances to indicate that he was looking for transportation.

Delemater fell in behind him, and because the man had no reason to believe he was being followed, the problem was a simple one. Sidewalk traffic was light and consisted mostly of neighborhood women, most of them with small children or baby carriages.

Not once in the next two blocks did the man glance over his shoulder. When he swung right at the next corner, Delemater had moved up until he was no more than fifty feet behind. The man crossed to the opposite side, and Delemater stayed where he was and kept abreast of him from his side of the street. At the next corner the man turned left again, but he was slowing down now and he seemed to be looking at numbers on the small apartment buildings that stood in a row on that side of the street.

Apparently he found the one he wanted in the middle of the block because he turned here, went up one step and past an open glass door into the entryway. Delemater stopped opposite him, wondering now as he considered his next step. Then, as he had done before, the man made further speculation unnecessary. In a matter of seconds he came back out of the doorway, and when Delemater saw the two envelopes in his hand, he had a pretty good answer about what had happened.

This was where Fay Novak lived. For reasons of her own, she was still reluctant to return and she had sent the man to pick up her mail. Now, as the other tucked the envelopes into an inside pocket and buttoned his topcoat, Delemater started back down the street ahead of the man, keeping the distance between them constant, turning left at the corner and slowing down a bit until he was sure the other was going to retrace his steps.

When he reached the tavern where he had had breakfast, he was about six paces in front of the man and he let him draw gradually closer until he reached a spot opposite the doorway Fay Novak had entered. By that time he had a cigarette between his lips and he took one more step and stopped to light it. He heard rather than saw the man turn behind him, his steps slowing now as he reached for the outer glass door. The entrance was at sidewalk level and Delemater let his head come round. Over the cupped hands that held the match he saw the man stop in front of the row of mailboxes on the right wall. He took a sideways step to get a better angle of vision. He watched the other punch the button below the fourth recessed box on the right and walk over to the inner door. After a short wait, he reached for the knob and pushed on inside.

Delemater threw the match away and grinned. He started back toward the tavern. A woman with a shopping bag in her hand gave him a second glance when she heard his soft humming, but he was not aware of this. There was a preoccupied look on his round face and he was thinking about the job he had done and wishing they could all be that simple. All he had to do now was get in touch with Casey, and the tavern was a nice quiet place to sit and study the *Racing Form* and get his bets lined up for the day.

16

LIEUTENANT LOGAN was behind his desk when Casey walked in at nine thirty that morning, but there was a harried expression on his lean face and his greeting was not exactly cordial. He glanced up from the papers spread out before him long enough to scowl, and there was a growling sound in his throat before he said:

"What do you want? I'm a busy man."

Casey ignored the comment. He knew how it was with Logan and could appreciate the pressure that was probably being applied by his superiors. But he had seen the lieutenant in similar moods before, and he thought it would wear off once he got him talking. He opened his coat, fanned it back, and sat down in the straight-backed chair at the end of the desk. He got a cigarette going; then for a silent thirty seconds he studied the blank wall he could see from the lone window. He knew that eventually Logan would look up and growl at him again. It took another minute, but it finally happened.

"What do you want?" he demanded as he threw down his pencil.

"I gave you a lead last night," Casey said. "I want to know what happened to it."

"What lead?"

"What did Donald Caldwell say about his car being outside that office building?"

"He says it wasn't."

"I saw it," Casey protested. "Do you think I made that license number up?"

"There's a garage under Caldwell's apartment," Logan said. "It has an attendant. Caldwell leaves his car there nights and sometimes during the day, but not always. Sometimes he parks it out on the street because it's more convenient. . . . What time did you see that car last night?"

"I don't know exactly."

"I can tell you when the call came in from Levy's office. Eight twenty-seven."

"Then I must have seen it about the same time."

"Caldwell says his car was parked out on the street near his apartment. He says he was there all evening. The garage man got a call from Caldwell around nine o'clock. Caldwell said he wasn't going to use the car and would the garage man go out and bring it in. The garage man did. He's done it before."

"So it's Caldwell's word against mine."

"For now anyway."

Casey considered the information and thought of something else. "Did you get a list of Levy's callers yesterday?"

Logan pawed through the papers on his desk and came up

with a typewritten list. He passed it over to Casey without comment. Casey scanned it and found only one name he recognized. This one bothered him, and the feeling of guilt that had been gnawing at his conscience came back again to infuse his thoughts. For the name was Frederick Babcock, and according to the list Babcock had kept an appointment with Julius Levy at five o'clock yesterday afternoon.

The fact that this notation might not have any special significance did not help. There was nothing to suggest that Babcock had come back later. In his own mind he was sure that he had seen Caldwell's car, but this in itself was no proof that Caldwell had seen Levy. The important thing was that so long as there was a possibility that either Caldwell, Babcock, or Eagan might have come back to look for those films, the lie he, Casey, had told would continue to haunt him.

"Do you still think Levy walked in on someone who was searching the office?"

"Yes," Logan said. "And both he and the guy who slugged him were unlucky."

"How?"

"It's like I told you last night. Levy was small-boned, delicate. They did an autopsy and found his skull was delicate, too. The medical examiner says he was hit by something with sharp edges, probably a gun. But the blow that killed him would probably have just bounced off a thick skull like yours."

"I still think there's a connection between Alpert and Levy," Casey said.

"Nobody's arguing with you on that, but from what I know about Clem Alpert, he was always on the take. A little blackmail would be routine for him. Levy's reputation says he wouldn't be mixed up in anything like that for a million bucks."

"That isn't what I meant," Casey said.

"Well, what the hell do you mean?"

"I think Johnny Keeler makes the connection," Casey said.

Logan leaned back, his eyes half-closed. "Well, go ahead," he said. "Convince me."

Casey pulled in his legs and sat up. He spoke again of the things he had seen the night Johnny Keeler had been stricken. He admitted that all he had was a hunch, but he mentioned the unlocked safe and the keys that were in it. He said the circumstances surrounding Alpert's murder made it seem likely that Alpert had taken some films from Keeler's safe and tried to cash in on them.

Logan did not argue the point. "Okay," he said. "Assume you're right—and it's a big assumption—how does Levy fit in?"

"Levy was Keeler's adviser. He could have known why Alpert was with Keeler the night he died. Alpert's office was searched either before or after he was killed. He went for a gun and missed, but you said he could have lived for ten or fifteen minutes after he was hit."

"So?"

"That's long enough to talk," Casey said. "The killer didn't get what he came after. Alpert could have told him that Levy had what he wanted. He might have known he was dying and wanted to get across the idea that the killer wasn't going to get away with it—"

Logan interrupted him. He took a big breath and let it out. "Oh, brother," he said. "Can't you do better than that?"

Casey knew what Logan meant. And now that he had the theory out in the open, it seemed highly improbable. The grin that began to work on his rugged face was a little sheepish, but he was too stubborn to discard the thought completely. The trouble was he could find no good way to substantiate it.

"Sure it's wild," he said. "But I still say there was some connection between Keeler and Alpert and his murder."

"I believe you."

Casey gave him a surprised squint, not sure he had heard right. "You do?"

"We found a check in Alpert's wallet for three hundred dollars," Logan said. "It was signed by Keeler. That sounds like a connection, doesn't it?"

"You didn't tell me," Casey said.

"There are lots of things I don't tell you."

"Levy could have known about that check."

"So?"

Casey gave up. He was aware of the futility of trying to sell Logan on an idea that he could not even sell himself, and as his mind moved on he thought again of Sam Delemater and wondered how he was doing.

"Did you find Fay Novak?"

"Not yet," Logan said glumly.

"Did you go over her apartment?"

"Certainly."

"Didn't you find anything?"

"Yeah, we found something. A bullet hole in the door."

Casey sat up a little straighter, and when he was sure that Logan was serious, he remembered the little gun he had found in Fay Novak's handbag.

"A bullet hole?"

"Low down," Logan said. "Fired from the inside. The slug we dug out of the hall wall was a .22. It's probably not important, but we'll pick her up. It's just a matter of time."

He drew his chair closer to the desk and picked up his pencil. He gave Casey a final look. Deep down in his eyes there was a gleam of amusement, but nothing showed on his face and his voice was sardonic.

"School's out," he said. "Take off, will you? I'm sitting here doing my work like a good boy. I'm thinking pretty good for me and trying to earn the money the taxpayers give me. So what happens? I'll tell you."

"I don't want to know."

"You come in here with a lot of silly chatter, and all I get out of it is a head full of confusion."

Casey stood up and grinned at his friend. What he had heard was very hard to refute and he admitted it. "Yeah," he said. "I'm a little confused myself."

"Go take some pictures," Logan said. "If you ever get a sound lead, come back."

Casey said he would. But when he went out, he was not thinking of taking pictures. He knew, as he crossed the outer office, that he was going to have to do some more cheating on the *Express* this morning because there were still a couple of things he had to do.

Flynn Enterprises occupied an entire floor in one of the city's more modern office buildings. Double glass doors opposite the elevators stood open when Casey arrived, and he stepped into a waiting room that had pine paneling, indirect lighting, and wall-to-wall carpeting. Two salesmen waited on leather upholstered benches, and the blonde who sat behind the antique desk near the center of the room was stylishly dressed and exceptionally attractive. She gave Casey a smile that was perhaps more practiced than genuine, as he took off his hat and stated his business.

"Mr. Garrett, please," he said. "Mr. Casey."

"From what company, Mr. Casey?"

"The *Morning Express*."

The name must have impressed her because her expression now showed a faint interest and she said: "Oh, just a moment, Mr. Casey. I'll see if he's in."

She picked up one of the two telephones and dialed three numbers, and it was either an exceptionally sensitive instrument or she had a unique way of speaking because, although Casey saw her lips move, her voice was barely audible.

"If you can wait a few minutes," she said when she hung up, "Mr. Garrett will see you."

Casey rewarded her with another approving grin and started to make a circuit of the room, stopping now and then to examine some photographs that pictured various construction jobs Flynn Enterprises had completed. There were also some racing pictures at tracks in which Flynn had interests. He had come to the picture that showed last year's professional football team when he heard his name called.

"Through that door, Mr. Casey," the blonde said, no longer quite so distant. "The third office on your right."

Stan Garrett's private office was not noticeably spacious, but his two windows overlooked most of the nearby rooftops and the walls were filled with photographs of well-known sports figures, many of them autographed. Garrett did not bother to rise, but his manner was affable and his good-looking face wore its customary smile as he said good morning and invited Casey to sit down.

"What's on your mind?"

Casey sat down, and now that he was faced with the question, he realized he had better give it some thought. He took his time lighting a cigarette and let the silence build, noting again the softness in Garrett's face that self-indulgence and the lack of exercise had put there, the blond wavy hair, which he decided was worn too long. He saw the big smile fade a little under his steady, thoughtful gaze. He waited until the petulance began to show before he spoke.

"It's about the two boxes of films Keeler left me."

"What about them?"

"They've been giving me some trouble."

"In what way?"

"A lot of people seem to want them, some of them pretty badly, from the way things have been going. Your boss, for one. So I thought I might as well come down here and tell you to lay off."

"Me?" Garrett exaggerated his look of surprise and his laugh was a little too loud. "You must be kidding."

"Your wife made a pitch for those films a year ago," Casey said and amplified on the information Alma Jensen had given him. "Maybe her father believed her and maybe he didn't, but he didn't fall for the story."

"If my wife went to her father to ask for any films, it was her idea, not mine."

"I doubt it. It doesn't add up that way to me."

"Maybe you don't add like I do."

"Your boss wanted a couple of those films," Casey said. "That much I know. I think he sent a punk up to Keeler's suite a year or so ago to break into that old safe but the guy bungled it. Keeler got a new safe and took some precautions so it wouldn't happen again, so Flynn tried another angle, using you and your wife. That didn't work either so he dropped the idea until Keeler died and you told him those two boxes of films had been left to me. So that night you sent a couple of hoods up to my place with a gun to pick up the boxes."

"Balls," said Garrett.

"They missed because I didn't have them," Casey said and went on to explain what had happened. "Last night a friend of mine and I cornered them," he said. "I took the locker key from the big one—Ostrowski—and got the films from the South Station locker where he'd put them when you found out you didn't have the right box."

"Who's Ostrowski?"

"Don't kid me," Casey said. "They work for you—Ostrowski and Vernon—and they admitted it. So you told your wife to try again and she came to the office. She told a pretty good story. I guess she figured a sentimental slob like me might fall for it, and maybe I would have if I hadn't already known too much about some of those negatives."

Garrett grunted softly, a disdainful sound. "You've been looking at too much television, Casey. If you had anything on those two hoods, whatever their names are, you would have turned them over to the cops."

Casey heard the door open as Garrett spoke, and he glanced around just in time to see John Flynn closing it. The thought that this was a coincidence vanished instantly when Flynn moved over and flipped the switch on the interoffice communicator on the desk. He understood then that this had been arranged so that Flynn could hear what had been said. Apparently Flynn had heard enough for now.

He said: "Hello, Casey," and sat down in the room's remaining chair, a stocky, competent-looking man with close-cropped graying brown hair and intelligent blue eyes. His face had a squarish muscular look, and there was something about the slant of his jaw that said this was an aggressive, tenacious, and possibly ruthless man.

"I've been listening in," he said. "I was curious to hear what you had to say and see if you had any threats in mind."

"No threats," Casey said. "But I'm glad you listened so I won't have to repeat anything."

"Okay. So let's get down to the nut of this thing. You've got the films?"

"Yes."

"What do you figure on doing with them?"

"Right now I think I'll burn them all," Casey said. "That way nobody gets hurt."

"Have you had any other offers?"

"One."

"From my three old college buddies, hunh?"

"That's right."

"I can beat their offer."

"I don't doubt it."

Flynn glanced out the window and a muscle bunched at the hinge of his jaw. When he looked back he cocked his head slightly and the blue eyes narrowed in thought.

"I've heard a lot of things about you," he said, "most of them good. You add pretty good, too. Everything I heard stacks up okay."

He glanced at Garrett. "I made Stan a proposition a year ago. Ten thousand for the films. He got his wife to make a pitch to her father, but it didn't work. When I heard about Keeler and knew you had the films, I told him the offer was still open. He tried a little muscle and that didn't work, and then he tried his wife again and still no dice." He tipped one hand and nothing changed in his face. "You've got this same offer, Casey. Ten grand. Cash."

Casey stood up, knowing that he could do no business here and not liking Flynn's easy arrogance.

"It isn't that simple any more," he said. "I'm thinking about murder now."

"Murder?" the narrowness went out of Flynn's eyes and his brows climbed. "Who got killed?"

"Julius Levy. And before that, a private detective named

Clem Alpert." Casey stopped with his hand on the doorknob.
He offered a brief and expurgated version of his theory and
said: "I don't care about Clem Alpert, but maybe I'm partly
responsible for what happened to Julius Levy and it bothers
me."

"Why should you feel responsible?"

"You wouldn't understand," Casey said. "Let's just say I'm
working on it. If I should happen to come up with anything,
I'll be in touch."

"Have you got anything special going for you?"

"I've got a little help, if that's what you mean," Casey said
and thought again about Sam Delemater.

"Call Stan when you get ready to move," Flynn said and
pointed a finger at Garrett. "He'll know how to get in touch
with me."

17

SAM DELEMATER had set up shop on his corner table in
the tavern, and when Casey walked in shortly before noon he
saw that the only thing missing was the office tin of bicarbonate of soda. The bar had opened some time earlier; the
familiar bourbon highball, half consumed, was at the detective's right elbow; and the table top was so cluttered with
Delemater's research material that when Casey brought a
beer over he had to clear a little place for his glass.

He had got the message at the *Express* and knew that Fay
Novak had been located. There had been nothing particularly
pressing in the way of photographic assignments, and after
he had left word that he would be out of touch for the next
couple of hours, he had driven directly here. Now, as he sat
down and claimed Delemater's attention, he asked for details

and the detective supplied them. The report, which was de-
tailed and accurate, pleased him, and he did not interrupt
until Delemater had finished.

"Okay," he said. "Nice work, Sam. You don't know the guy,
hunh?"

"Never saw him before in my life."

"Describe him."

"Sort of big. About your size. A little younger maybe.
Rugged. Healthy looking, like he was used to working out-
doors. I'd say he was a country boy."

"Why?"

"His clothes. They were all right, you understand, but the
topcoat looked a little tight, like he wasn't used to wearing
it very often, and the hat brim was a little wide for a city
boy. If I had to make a guess, I'd say he was a farmer."

"He acted toward her as if they were friends?"

"Good friends."

"She sent him to her place for the mail, and he got two
letters."

"There could have been three or four," Delemater said, "but
I know there were two."

Casey thought it over and finished his beer before he stood
up.

"Are you happy here?"

Delemater glanced up, brow puckering good naturedly, as
he tried to analyze the remark.

"Sure."

"Okay." Casey grinned at him. "Stay put. I'll be back after
I've talked to her. . . ."

The fourth mailbox from the right in the apartment entryway had a card on it which said: *McMahon*. Casey tried the
inner door first, but when he found it locked he came back
and put his thumb on the button below the mailbox. After
a moment he heard the distorted sound of Fay Novak's voice
in the speaking tube.

"Yes?"

"Fay? This is Casey. I want to talk to you."

"I'm sorry." There was a pause. "This is Miss McMahon's apartment."

"I know that," Casey said. "I want to talk to you."

"Talk to who?"

"Fay Novak," Casey said, a mild exasperation coloring his tone.

"I'm sorry, there's no Fay Novak here."

"Cut it out," Casey yelled. "I know you're there because I had you followed. I don't want to have to call the police—yet. I'd rather talk to you first, but I'm not going to crowd you if you're not going to listen. Come on, push the button and unlock the door."

He moved away as he finished, and a second or two later there was a buzzing sound and he could hear the lock release. He pushed on inside, climbed one flight of stairs, and moved along the hall to a door on the right. It opened as soon as he knocked, and he saw that Fay Novak wore the same dark-red dress he had seen before, but with less makeup on her face she seemed younger and somehow more attractive. The room itself was small and had a feminine, cluttered look, but Casey was only vaguely aware of this as he fastened his glance on the big man in the gray suit who stood waiting in the center of the room. He found no fault with Delemater's description, for the outdoor look was certainly stamped upon the face and the gray-blue eyes had a watchful but somehow ingenuous look as the girl moved back to his side.

"Dan, this is Mr. Casey, an old friend of mine. . . . Mr. Hallmann."

Hallmann offered his hand and Casey found it hard and muscular. "Hello, Mr. Hallmann."

"I'm pleased to meet you, Mr. Casey," Hallmann said. "Any friend of Fay's is a friend of mine." He glanced fondly down at the girl and his smile was broad and genuine. "Does Mr. Casey know about us?" He put his arm lightly about her shoulder as he spoke and, ignoring the sudden pinkness in her cheeks and the confusion in her glance, he added proudly: "Fay and I are practically engaged, Mr. Casey."

The announcement was as surprising as it was unexpected.

It left Casey both confused and momentarily speechless, and the girl was no help because she kept her glance averted. Hallmann was still smiling down at her, and if he felt any embarrassment it did not show; instead there seemed to be an odd humbleness in his voice as he continued.

"Isn't that so, honey?"

"I guess so, Dan." The answer was soft and unexpectedly demure for one who had seen so much of life, and then, as though suddenly aware of this herself, her chin came up and her eyes were defiant and challenging. "Yes, we are."

"Wonderful," Casey said, a little incredulous but finding some words at last. He offered his hand again. "Congratulations, Mr. Hallmann."

"Well, she hasn't said yes yet," Hallmann said, "but I think she will."

Casey glanced at the girl again. Then, not knowing how else to do it, he spoke directly.

"I wonder if you'd excuse us for a few minutes, Mr. Hallmann. There are a couple of business matters I'd like to discuss with Fay. Privately, if you don't mind."

"Business matters?" Hallmann said uncertainly.

"That's right. Unfinished business." He paused until the girl looked at him, and his dark gaze was steady and determined as he continued. "Haven't you got some errands that Mr. Hallmann could do, Fay?" he asked. "Or maybe he could walk around the block and look the neighborhood over for a few minutes."

"All right," she said, realizing from Casey's attitude that he intended to stay until he had said what he had on his mind. "Mr. Casey works for a newspaper, Dan," she said. "There are a couple of things we'd like to talk about. Oh, they don't concern you and me."

"Yes," Casey said. "Just a couple of little things that ought to be cleared up."

For the first time Hallmann's eyes clouded, and his expression said he did not like what he had heard but did not quite know what to do about it.

"Well—I don't know—"

Fay Novak went over and picked up his hat and coat. She offered them to him. "Please, Dan, it won't take long." Then, moving close and pressing her body against him, she gave him an upward slanting glance that was both provocative and pleading. "Please?"

The approach was too much for Hallmann's resistance. He seemed momentarily tongue-tied but the spell had been cast by an expert in the game of coquetry and he obviously liked that sort of attention. What Fay wanted, Fay was probably going to get if she played her cards right, and the immediate reaction substantiated the thought.

"Sure, honey," he said, and now the smile came back and his manner was at once expansive. "If you want to talk to Mr. Casey in private, that's what you're going to do. Will ten or fifteen minutes be enough?"

The girl looked at Casey and he nodded imperceptibly and she told Hallmann that would be fine. She smiled at him and walked with him to the door, but when he had closed it the smile went away and her eyes were quickly troubled.

"How did you find me?"

Casey told her.

"Have you told the police?"

"Not yet. I didn't know where you were until just now."

"The story in the papers said they were looking for an attractive blonde—the newspapers always make the missing woman attractive, don't they?—and I suppose that's me. Why should they want me anyway?"

"They're wondering about that bullet hole in your door."

"I thought maybe they'd guess what made that hole."

"You really were running away from some guy that night, weren't you?"

"I told you I was."

"But it wasn't any ardent admirer from the Parkview who had had too much to drink."

"I just made that up."

"You did okay."

"I had to tell you something."

"It wasn't Hallmann?"

"Good God, no."

"Who is he? He sounded pretty serious talking about marrying you."

"He is serious."

"And what about you?"

"If I ever get out of this mess and he still wants me, the answer is going to be yes."

She moved over to a studio couch with a flowered slipcover and eased down on the edge of it. A frown was working on the penciled brows and she reached for the pack of cigarettes on the coffee table in front of her. When she put the cigarette between her lips Casey gave her a light and she sat there hunched over a little, forearms on her knees and distance in her gaze.

"He came into the cocktail lounge at the Parkview a couple of months ago."

"Who?"

"Dan Hallmann. He was sitting at a small table against the wall. He had one drink—this was before dinner—and to me he was just another customer. He came in again about ten o'clock and had one more drink. I wouldn't have noticed him at all except that he ordered ginger ale with his bourbon and not many people do. He was back the next night; same table, same time. He had one drink before dinner and one drink after dinner and each time he left a fifty-cent tip, which was twice what he should have left. These overtippers are sometimes looking for an opening and I wondered about him, but I didn't see him again until the following weekend."

She tapped ashes into a tray and said: "He was there Friday at dinner time. Same routine, except this time he said good evening and gave me a smile. Same thing on Saturday night. He didn't make any passes or any propositions, but I was aware of him now and I could tell that he was watching me work whenever he was in the room. By that time I was pretty curious. He didn't look like any of the regulars. I didn't think he was a salesman or smart-aleck city character; he looked more like a hick, but a nice hick. I was pretty sure by then that he was working up to something but I could tell he was shy, and it took him four weeks before he got nerve enough to ask if he could take me home." She put the cigarette out and looked at Casey, her smile twisted but genuine.

"I knew what I was going to say before he asked me," she said. "I hadn't had an approach like that since I was a kid and I had to know what made him tick. I said yes, and he asked if I'd like to stop somewhere for something to eat, and I was ready for that, too. I wanted to find out how he handled himself when he was out and how he'd react when he found out he had to spend a little. I told him I'd like to go to the Club Leon, so we went. I had two drinks and a sandwich, and it was Saturday night, with a cover charge, and the check was fourteen fifty. If the tab bothered him, it didn't show. He left a good tip and took me home and gave me a very polite and gentlemanly good-night at my door."

Her smile changed as she paused again. It was more open and revealing.

"By that time he had me half-hooked," she said and laughed softly. "I'd found out quite a lot about him, too."

She went on quickly then, a new brightness in her glance, and what she said as she continued was further proof of Sam Delemater's astuteness.

"He's thirty-seven years old. He's never been married. Worked hard all his life because his father sort of dominated him. But the father died a couple of years ago and Dan was the only child and the old man did pretty well by him. He has a farm down in Rhode Island, not a regular farm, I guess, but he raises fancy-bred cows or cattle or something like that. He says the place overlooks the bay and he has a small boat and a man to look after things while he's away so he can go to Florida for a couple of months in the winter. He's really in love with me," she added, looking round at Casey now. "I know that now for sure."

"I take it he's asked you to marry him."

"Last week."

"What did you tell him?"

"I told him I was very fond of him and I thought it would work out but I had to think it over. I told him I'd let him know this week."

"What's there to think over?"

"A lot of things," she said, her tone again thoughtful. "I've been going along these last few years getting nowhere, always looking for some break I didn't deserve, telling myself that next month or next year things would be better. I had a marriage that didn't work out, and I've been earning my own living ever since I was seventeen. I guess I've done some things I'm ashamed of, but nothing really very bad. I finally realized, when I made myself think, that my trouble was I'm lazy. I guess a girl is always looking for some fellow to get her out of the rut and give her a home and affection and a chance for some happiness."

Her face twisted as she paused, and for a second or two she fought to keep back the tears.

"I'm tired of scrambling for a dollar and always cutting corners and doing things I hate so I can get the rent money. I'm fed up with living alone and fighting off propositions from traveling salesmen, and taking a half hour to slap on my makeup and fix my face and worry about my hair." With the tips of her fingers she gave an irritable flip to the tinted blonde hair.

"With Dan I can let it grow out the way it should. It's brown naturally, and what's wrong with that? I told him he wouldn't like me the way I really am and he said he would like me better and I think maybe he would. I'm twenty-eight years old and I finally got a chance to have a home and maybe a couple of kids, but I'm not going to start out on the wrong foot. I've been trying to work up nerve to tell him how it has been with me. I had to stall him last weekend because I'd promised to do something and I didn't know how to get out of it. But I want to pull the curtain down on the old Fay Novak, and if he loves me enough I think he'll believe me."

"So do I," Casey said. Then, because there were other things that had to be said before Hallmann came back, he spoke of the letters the man had brought from her apartment.

"You must have been expecting something special."

She looked at him again and the smile was gone. A new tightness began to work on her mouth, and as the silence started to build, he pressed for an answer.

"Where are they now?"

"I have them."

"One of those letters must be very important."

"I guess it is."

"Who sent it?"

Silence came again, and to break it, Casey made an educated guess.

"Was there a film or films in that envelope?"

"Why—yes," she said, her surprise showing.

"Did Keeler take them?"

"Yes."

"Then they belong to me," Casey said and explained the provisions in Keeler's will.

"That will says any and all films Keeler had are mine. . . . Come on, Fay," he pressed. "We haven't got much time. You're going to have to come clean with Hallmann, and you know it. If you're smart, you can do it in your own way and in your own time. If you're going to hold out on me, I've got to get the police over here right now."

The threat had the desired effect, and Fay Novak stood up and walked into the adjoining bedroom. When she came back she had her handbag open, and a glance at the envelope she gave him was sufficient to tell him that the return address consisted of a post-office-box number imprinted in the upper left-hand corner.

"Is that Clem Alpert's box number?" he asked, deciding he might as well make another guess.

She nodded silently, the tightness still in her face, and he held the envelope up to the light before he tore off one end. Inside was a four-frame strip of thirty-five-millimeter film, but even when he inspected it closely he found the images too small to identify. The only thing he knew for sure was that they were interior scenes.

"Do you know what they are?"

"Yes," she said. "But I'm not going to tell you. You're a photographer. Print them and then you'll know."

Casey inserted the film in the envelope and put it back into his pocket.

"Who did you run from the other night?"

She shook her head and remained mute.

"You know who it was, though."

"Maybe."

"Why did you have to shoot?"

"He was trying to get in," she said. "He was trying to unlock the door and I wanted to let him know I had a gun."

"Then what?"

"I was still scared," she said. "I was afraid to go to bed. I was afraid I'd fall asleep and he might come back. I decided that would be worse than trying to get out so I took a chance. I had no idea where I was going, I couldn't even think. I just kept walking and I saw this place and I went in to get a drink and you were there."

"Yeah."

"I could see right off I couldn't talk you into letting me use your place and then I remembered my friend. Luckily she was in and she said she was going out of town for two or three days and I was welcome to stay here. I stayed with her that first night and she left the next morning. I've been here ever since. . . ."

The knock at the door stopped her, and she gave a small but audible gasp. She seemed to have a moment of panic and there was a trapped look in her eyes. Casey, understanding this, took her arm and gave it a small shake. He spoke quickly, keeping his voice low but reassuring.

"It's okay, Fay," he said. "I'm going to have to tell Lieutenant Logan about you because I can't hold out on him now. But there'll be time for you to have your talk with Hallmann.

He seems like a pretty decent guy, so why not give him a chance to prove it. It'll work out."

He had been crossing the room as he spoke, and now he opened the door and Hallmann entered, his glance darting past Casey to the girl.

"Did I come back too soon?"

"No," Casey said, "I was just leaving."

"Good." Hallmann offered a tentative smile and looked relieved. "Is everything all right?"

"Just fine," Casey said. "Right, Fay?"

"Yes," the girl said. "Just fine."

"She's been telling me about you," Casey said. "I'd say you were a pretty lucky guy."

"I think so, too," Hallmann said and gave Casey another of his strong hard handclasps. "Yes, indeed, Mr. Casey. And thank you for your good wishes."

He started toward the girl, and as Casey went out, he made a small circle with his thumb and forefinger behind the man's back. When he was sure Fay Novak saw the signal, he gave her an added nod of encouragement.

18

SAM DELEMATER was happily at work with his racing statistics at the corner table when Casey came back to the tavern. He glanced up, grinned, and finished what was left of his highball.

"I think I've got me a sleeper," he said. "In the sixth at Gulfstream."

"Great," Casey said, a touch of sarcasm in his voice. "You pick sleepers while I pay you forty-five bucks a day."

"I also work while I pick them."

"Work? How?"

"Be patient, son, and I'll show you." He pushed his chair

back and began to arrange the papers on the table in a neat pile. When he was satisfied he put on his coat and hat. He folded the papers and stuffed them into his topcoat pocket. "Here," he said and drew Casey over to the window with the open Venetian blind. "I think you had a tail on you when you got here."

Casey scowled at him. "You're kidding."

"I don't think so."

"Why would anyone follow me?"

"I am not psychic yet," Delemater said. "I only know what I see. . . . That guy holding up the wall between the drugstore and the tobacco shop."

Casey saw the man as Delemater spoke. He appeared to be reading a folded newspaper, but from this distance all Casey could tell was that he was reasonably tall and wore a gray topcoat and a light-gray hat. He also knew that this was no one he had ever seen before, and as he tried to find some reason why the man should be here, Delemater continued.

"What do you want to do about him?"

"I'd like to know who sent him."

"That won't be too easy," Delemater said. "I doubt if he's going to volunteer anything and we can't get too rough in broad daylight."

"Maybe we could find out who he is. If we are both neat and quick we might get a look at his wallet."

"It's possible," Delemater conceded. "You want to brace him and try?"

"Let's."

They left the tavern together and crossed the street at the corner. As they did so, the man in the gray hat lowered the paper and moved out to stand at the curb. He kept his glance turned deliberately the other way, and although he must have heard them walk behind him, he did not turn until it was too late.

They took him from each side and for a few seconds he might as well have been in a vise. They pinned his arms and leaned hard, holding him immobile while Casey slid one hand inside the coat and lifted the wallet. He heard the man say: "Hey," and then he had the wallet open and was inspecting the photostat of a private detective's license made out to one William Rogovin and giving a New York City address. As he held it out to give Delemater a glance, Rogovin found his voice.

"What the hell is this? What do you think you're doing?"

"Be quiet, friend," Delemater said, releasing his grip. "You're causing a disturbance."

Casey returned the wallet.

"Who hired you?" He did not expect an answer so he looked at Delemater. "Mr. Rogovin is a colleague of yours, Sam."

"So I noticed," Delemater said. "How are things in the big city, friend?"

"Go to hell."

Delemater made clucking noises with his tongue, and though his small grin was fixed, his gray gaze was hard and intent.

"If you have any business here, state it; if not, take a walk."

"When I'm ready," Rogovin blustered. "If you're a town cop, let's see your buzzer."

"I'll tell you what," Delemater said. "You don't belong in this neighborhood, so suppose we call you a cab."

"I don't want a cab. I'm staying here."

"That's what you think."

Delemater gave Casey a small nod and together they closed in on Rogovin again, making no fuss but walking him stiff-legged and resisting to the curb on Spring Street with a minimum of fuss. Delemater hailed the first taxi that came along. When it stopped he opened the door and gave Rogovin his instructions.

"You can get in quietly and roll," he said softly, "or you can give us an argument. If that's the way you want it we'll be glad to oblige and take our chances with the law."

Rogovin hesitated, but not for long. He seemed about to challenge the ultimatum, hesitated, and, as though he saw something in Delemater's face that told him further resistance might be a poor idea, he was lost. Jerking his arm loose, he summoned what dignity he could and climbed into the back seat. Delemater shut the door.

"Tell the driver where you want to go," he said. "Just don't come back."

They watched the cab roll off and Delemater looked rather pleased with himself until he saw the frown working around Casey's dark eyes.

"Have you got any idea who hired him?"

"I've got an idea," Casey said and changed the subject. "Are you carrying a gun?"

"I don't carry a gun once in six months any more."

"Then get one."

Delemater cocked his head, his eyes prying until he realized Casey was not kidding.

"Is something going to happen?"

"I don't know," Casey said, "but you're a handy man to have around, Sam, and I want to be sure you earn that dough I'm paying you."

"Have you got anything special in mind?"

"I don't know that either," Casey said. "But I found out some things this morning. For the first time in the last couple of days I also started to do some proper thinking. Get the gun and some lunch and come to my place when you can. Say two or two-thirty, or whenever you can make it. Maybe by that time I'll know how to crack this thing."

"And what're you going to be doing for now?"

"I'm a little worried about Fay Novak," Casey said and knew this was the truth. "I don't know why this private dick followed me or what he's after, but I ought to give Fay the word."

He turned as he spoke and started down the street, going into the apartment entrance and again pressing the button under the card that said *McMahon*. When Fay Novak's voice came to him he spoke his piece.

"This is Casey again, Fay," he said. "Just listen and don't argue. I found out somebody followed me here this morning and it worries me a little. I don't know what it means either, but I don't think you should take any chances. Has Hallmann got a room at the Parkview?"

"Why, yes."

"All right. Go there. I don't care what you tell him, but I want him to stay with you, have you got that?"

"Yes, but—"

"No buts. Get Hallmann to take you over to his room and stay with him. I mean keep him there at least for this afternoon. You didn't tell me all you knew, but I'm beginning to get a picture and I don't like it. Now are you going to be a good girl and do what I ask?"

"All right, Jack."

"Good," Casey said. "I'll be in touch with you later. If I don't call you by six, call me at my place."

Casey had the boxes of films on his mind when he unlocked the downstairs door of the apartment at two-thirty that afternoon, but it had been his intention to take his camera and equipment bag up to his rooms before he went down to the cellar. That he changed his mind was due to the position of the door that led downstairs. Instead of being closed as it normally was, one edge projected into the hall, and he saw that it was ajar.

He had no premonition that anything was wrong at the time. It was, he knew, a door that was seldom used, but not until he noticed the crack of light that showed in the opening did he begin to wonder who was down there. Had it not been for the fact that those negatives were already in his thoughts, he might not have investigated, but as it was, he opened the door still more and stepped onto the landing.

"Hello," he called, directing his voice down the narrow stairwell and noticing that there was no other light on below. "Anybody down there?"

There was no answer to this so he called again; then, assuming that the last person down there had forgotten to switch off the light, he turned it off himself. He came back to the hall and here he stopped, his hand still on the knob, as an odd feeling of doubt and uncertainty began to work on him. When he could no longer ignore it, he put down his camera and bag, stepped back on the landing, and again turned on the light.

No longer trying to justify his actions, he started down. By that time he had to be sure about those negatives and, still not having any sense that anything was wrong, he reached the concrete floor and started to grope for the dangling cord that he knew hung from the ceiling socket somewhere to one side.

It was dark and his eyes had not yet adjusted so that he saw nothing at all as his fingers found the cord. It was then that instinct came to his aid and told him something was wrong. A new and unaccountable alertness was suddenly upon him, and he unconsciously stiffened and held his breath.

He tried to penetrate the darkness. There was nothing to see in the surrounding emptiness but now, with his hearing sharply tuned, he thought he heard some whisper of sound at one side. For another second he stood tense and immobile, and then he knew that what he heard did not come from any outward movement but was the soft sound of breathing not his own. At the same time he became aware of a new odor that was not part of the cellar.

Then, convinced that he had company, he moved, not pulling the light cord, not knowing what danger might await him, but lunging sideways and reaching out with one hand as he drew the other back.

He went in with a slight crouch, and his outstretched hand found a coat sleeve. Momentum bumped him into the unseen body, and he heard a frightened cry. Something metallic clattered to the floor. As his other arm encircled a waist, its softness told him that this was a woman, and the odor was in his nostrils now, the perfumed essence suddenly strong. With that, he stepped away and reached again for the cord, but his hands and arms were left with an impression of her body, and its size told him who it was before the light went on.

He had to blink to adjust to the new brightness, and it was worse for Alma Jensen because she had been in the darkness longer. She stood very still as she fought to regain her composure, her strong body erect in the camel's hair coat, her head bare, her handsome face pale at the cheekbones.

The green eyes grew enormous as they focused on Casey, and he looked around to see what it was she had dropped. The metallic noise he had heard had been made by a screwdriver, and as he stooped to pick it up, he saw that the blade was bent. When he stepped to the storage crib he saw the marks on the wooden frame and understood that she had been trying to pry the staple out so she could open the door.

By then he knew why she had come and what she wanted. There were still a lot of questions milling around inside his head, but the answer to one—how she knew the films were here in the first place—came to him now as he remembered that he had confided in her the night before when he had gone to her apartment.

"Where did you get this?" he asked, indicating the screwdriver.

"Over there." She pointed to a work bench dimly visible against a far wall.

"You were down here working in the dark?" he asked when he had returned the screwdriver.

"Not at first," she said. "I had to have the light on to find out which was the proper storage room. After that, I turned the light off because I was afraid someone might notice it."

"How did you get in the house?"

"I had some keys," she said. "They worked all right in the front door, but none of them fitted the padlock."

"I guess you wanted the films," Casey said, still a little amazed at what had happened and not fully understanding the reasons for her attempt. "Why?"

"I was worried about them. It's hard to explain. I think if I had got them I would have destroyed them. I guess that sounds pretty silly."

"It's not the word I'd use."

"No, I suppose it is rather inadequate. But whatever word you want to use, it's the truth."

Casey found his keys and unlocked the door. He took out the two film boxes, tucked them under his arm, and relocked the door. He pointed to the stairs and waited until she reached them before he turned off the light. He followed her up and into the hall. He closed the door and glanced down at his camera and equipment bag and somewhere up above him he thought he heard the distant sound of a bell. As he listened, another sound came to him from the entryway, and when he stepped over and opened the door Sam Delemater was standing there.

"I've been ringing your bell for three minutes," the detective said. "Why didn't you let me in?"

"I'm letting you in now," Casey said. "Come on."

Delemater entered, glanced at Alma Jensen, and then took a better look. Quick approval touched his gray eyes as he inspected her face, and a grin began to work at the corners of his mouth. When Casey was a little slow in making the introduction he cleared his throat and stepped forward.

"You're Mrs. Jensen, aren't you?" he said and offered his hand. "I'm Sam Delemater."

"Hello, Mr. Delemater."

"This is a real pleasure," Delemater said and sounded as if he meant it.

"Let's go upstairs," Casey said. "Get my camera and bag, will you, Sam?"

Once they were in his living room, Casey invited them to take off their coats. He said they might be here a while and why not be comfortable.

"You've got something planned?" Delemater asked.

Casey considered the question as he put the two boxes of films on the mantelpiece. For he had been busy since he had left the detective on the corner by the tavern. He had taken time to eat a bowl of soup and a sandwich, and while he ate, the ideas he had picked up here and there that morning began to crystallize. He had taken the four-frame strip of thirty-five-millimeter film to the studio and slipped it into the enlarger. He did not want to bother with prints with other photographers around, but he adjusted the enlarger so he could project eight-by-ten images upon a plain piece of white paper and what he saw was sufficient for him to understand exactly what those films contained.

This knowledge told him he was on the right track, and he had scouted around the editorial floor until he found an empty office and a telephone. It took him a little while to reach the people he wanted, but the invitations he issued were in the nature of a command performance. What he had to say got immediate attention. Those who listened were both intrigued and impressed, and he phrased his requests in such a way that refusal was difficult. Now, as he put his camera and equipment bag in the closet, he knew that the meeting should be getting under way in another half hour or so.

"Yes," he said, answering Delemater. "But there are a few things to do before the meeting comes to order. You know how to make enlargements from thirty-five-millimeter negatives, don't you?"

"Sure. If you set things up for me, I can handle it okay."

Casey took the envelope from his pocket and removed the film he had taken from Fay Novak. He showed it to Alma Jensen and told her where he got it. Her only reaction was a small nod, and he led her over to a chair by the window and told her to sit down. He asked her if she would like a drink. When she said no, he said he would be right back.

In the darkroom he got out his trays and developer and hypo. He fitted the negatives into the enlarger and adjusted it so it was properly focused to make four-by-five prints. He showed Delemater how the timer worked and told him what printing paper to use.

"These don't have to be permanent prints," he said. "Give them enough hypo to set them for a while and wash them a bit and then put them on the ferrotyper. Later we can make other prints with the full treatment, but hang onto that film."

Back in the living room, he went immediately to the fireplace. There was a large antique copper bucket at one side which served as his wood box, and he took the three small logs it contained and laid them on the andirons. He took the stone from the Cape Cod lighter, let the excess kerosene drip off, worked it into the ashes, and then lit it.

Alma Jensen had settled herself comfortably in the club chair, with her coat off. She was smartly clad in a flannel skirt and a cashmere sweater set. She sat with crossed knees and the leg which was exposed from the kneecap down was very shapely indeed. Her face was composed now; the green eyes were at ease as they watched Casey pull the ladder-back chair away from the kneehole desk and sit down close to her.

He offered cigarettes and she accepted, bending forward to get a light. She inhaled and leaned back, and he scowled a moment at the tip of his cigarette before he spoke.

"Do you know Fay Novak?"

"I know who she is."

"You saw that strip of film?"

"Yes."

He explained how he happened to have it in his possession and how Fay had got the envelope in the mail.

"Do you know what's on it?"

"Not really."

"But you could guess."

"I could guess, yes."

"You assumed that strip was in one of those two boxes."

"Yes, I suppose I did."

"If you had managed to get away with those two boxes, you would have destroyed it."

"Yes. At least that's what I thought I'd do."

"Why?"

"I tried to explain that to you the other night. With Johnny gone, there was no longer any point in having that film around. At least, I didn't want to have the responsibility."

"So you lied to me a little."

"A little."

"You knew what Johnny was doing Saturday night. You knew why he was with Clem Alpert."

"Yes."

"That's why you stopped at his place late. To see what had happened." He hesitated. When she did not reply, he said: "You didn't approve of the idea, did you?"

"No. Neither did Julius Levy. I said so, but it didn't do any good. Johnny was stubborn about a lot of things and this was one of them. He'd had it on his mind a long time, but only he and the doctor knew that he was a sick man. He must have known that there was always a chance that there would be a stroke or a hemorrhage and it would be fatal. He wanted to do this thing before that happened."

Casey considered her remarks, and when he saw there was nothing more he could add, he rose and went over to the mantelpiece. The tape was still on the two boxes where Julius Levy had sealed them and now he removed it. He took off the covers and looked at the contents, which had been arranged in Keeler's own way. He had seen the collection once before, when he had stopped at Keeler's suite while the older man was bringing his filing system up to date, and it looked the same now.

The first half of one box contained four-by-five glass plates which had been made early in Keeler's career before film became so universally accepted. The balance of that box contained four-by-five and two-and-a-quarter by three-and-a-quarter films, each one separated by a thin card which bore a number. There were also tabs which separated certain sections and gave a clue regarding the nature of the negatives. These were marked: *Action—Sports—Nudes—Spot News— Human Interest,* and whatever other categories had come to Keeler's mind.

The second box contained the smaller negatives—two-and-a-quarter by two-and-a-quarter and thirty-five millimeter. Here a cardboard divider ran down the center lengthwise. This saved space, and each small negative was by itself with a paper separator bearing a number. At the back of the box was a small leather-covered notebook containing a cross index and listing the numbers which identified each film. The system might have been confusing to an outsider, but Keeler knew how to lay his hands on the negative he wanted and that was good enough for him.

Satisfied now that all was in order, Casey put the two boxes on the floor near the hearth. He stepped toward the darkroom and pushed the door open to ask Delemater how he was doing. When the detective said he was almost finished Casey knew he was as ready as he was going to be for the guests he had invited, with one exception. Remembering this now, he went to the telephone and dialed the number of police headquarters.

He had tried this number before he left the office, and the answer he got from the detective who spoke to him was the same as the one he had heard before. Logan was out.

"I called him before," Casey said. "I left word for him."

"I don't know about that," the detective said. "I wasn't here."

"Don't you know where he is?"

"No. Probably having his meal. All I know is he's not here now."

"Well, when he comes back or calls in," Casey said, "if he ever does, give him a message, will you? Tell him Casey called twice."

"I'll tell him."

"Tell him if he can find the time he should come to my place as soon as he can."

"I said I'd tell him," the detective said. "Or leave word for him. Anything else?"

"Just tell him it could be important. He may not like my party, but I don't want him going around saying he wasn't invited."

19

DISTRICT ATTORNEY T. J. EAGAN was the first to arrive. His squarish face still had the gamecock set to the jaw and his eyes were busy and tinged with suspicion as Casey closed the door and said that he would take Eagan's hat and coat. The district attorney surrendered them without comment and was properly introduced to Alma Jensen. But his glance had caught the objects which were of interest to him, and he moved over to the two metal boxes on the floor and glanced down at them.

"Those are Keeler's films, hunh?"

"Yes."

"All of them?"

"All of them."

"So what do I do now?"

"Go over there and sit down, Mr. Eagan," Casey said and waved him toward the davenport. "You should have company any minute now."

Donald Caldwell and Fred Babcock came in together shortly after Eagan had seated himself, Caldwell with his rich man's tan on the unlined face and balding head, Babcock lanky and sober-faced now but somehow distinguished-looking. They, too, surrendered their hats and coats and were introduced to Alma Jensen. They saw the two open boxes of films but said nothing, and as they started to join Eagan, the knock came again at the door and Casey went over to admit Big John Flynn and Stanley Garrett. Their nods were abrupt and reserved as they recognized the trio on the davenport, and by the time they were seated in the matching wingchairs, Delemater came out of the darkroom with four prints in his hand.

"Do you want these?" he asked.

"Keep them for now," Casey said and introduced him to the five men. "Sam's probably the best private detective in town," he added by way of elaboration. "He's been giving me a hand on some things."

Casey waited until Delemater sat down near the door. He was thinking hard now as he groped for some way to start because he knew there were a lot of things he had to say and he wanted to be sure the points he made registered. He glanced at Stan Garrett, who had slumped a little in his chair and was trying to look bored without too much success. He found Flynn watching him with narrowed eyes and he could see the annoyance on the blunt, strong-boned face. In the end it was he who spoke as Casey continued to grope.

"I'm not sure what this is all about," he said flatly, "but I haven't got too much time. So call the meeting to order, Casey. We're all here, aren't we?"

"I've been trying to get Lieutenant Logan—"

"Logan?" Eagan leaned forward. "He's a homicide man, isn't he?"

"That's right."

"So how does he fit?" Flynn said.

"Before we get through with this session," Casey said, "we might need a homicide man around." He gave them a moment to let the words sink in. "I thought it might be a good idea to call him."

"We came to talk about those films," Caldwell said. "At least that's what you led me to believe."

"We're going to talk about those films," Casey said. "It may take a while, and you'll have to bear with me. I can serve drinks later, but Mr. Flynn's got a point. Let's get down to business."

He put an elbow on the edge of the mantelpiece and said: "Every one of you is interested in some of these negatives and I asked you here because I wanted you to know just what's going to happen to them. You already know about Keeler's will and how I got them. A letter was left with those boxes and I want you to hear it. I want you to understand how he felt about those negatives because his thoughts certainly influenced me when I found out they were going to make trouble."

He read the letter and his audience was attentive and made no interruption. When he finished he pointed to the three piles of plate-negatives he had arranged carefully on the mantelpiece, each with its paper divider.

"I've only looked at a couple of these, but they're old and I'm going to take Keeler's advice. They could be useful. They might have considerable value to students and researchers from a historical standpoint. I'm going to call the Public Library and the University Library and decide what should be done with them. If nobody wants them, I may keep some of them myself."

He paused and hunkered down beside the two boxes. "That leaves these films," he said. "It also explains this fire, which I didn't start to make the room look more cheerful. Films burn quickly," he added to make sure they got the idea. "Maybe they should have been burned long ago. Keeler's letter says he had the same idea from time to time but he was so attached to them, and had had them for so long, he couldn't make himself do it. It's like a man who has to lose an arm, I guess. He can't cut it off himself, but it's all right if someone else does it for him. With these films, I'm the one who got stuck."

Flynn was the first to reply. As Casey reached for a handful of negatives, he said: "My offer still goes."

"You're outvoted," Casey said. "Three to one." He took time to glance at the three men on the davenport. "Am I right?"

"You are," said Eagan and the others nodded.

"You want to cause trouble, Mr. Flynn," Casey said. "I don't. I want to prevent anyone from getting hurt by anything I do." Again he directed his glance at the davenport. "I'm giving no films away; to you or anyone else. But if your story was true, this should satisfy you."

He tossed the films into the blazing logs and watched them curl and dissolve and tinge the flames with blue. He took another handful, and another. When the first box was empty

Flynn stood up, his face flushed and his jaw muscles bulging.

"Get my hat and coat," he said, "and I'll be on my way. You can finish the rest of the fireworks later."

"If you say so," Casey said. "But I have another set of negatives you might be interested in."

Flynn considered the remark as he stood in front of his chair. He took a minute to give Casey a long and thoughtful stare and the room was quiet while he made up his mind and glanced at his wrist watch.

"All right," he said finally and sat down again. "I've got a few minutes. Get on with the act."

Casey continued to burn the films. When he finished he put the covers on the empty boxes and placed one on top of the other. This done, he straightened up and looked at Delemater.

"Have you got that filmstrip, Sam?"

"I left it in the enlarger."

"Will you get it, please?"

Delemater went out to the darkroom and came back with the strip of film in his hand. He gave it to Casey, but before anything more could be said someone knocked on the door. Delemater glanced at Casey, got a small nod, and went over to open it.

There was a stormy look on Lieutenant Logan's lean dark face as he started into the room with Sergeant Manahan at his shoulder. Casey recognized that look and knew that under other circumstances Logan would have given voice to certain complaints. As it was, he counted the roll quickly and was apparently impressed by the quality of the guests. His glance lingered longest on District Attorney Eagan and he quickly accepted the fact that he was outranked. Still not knowing what this was all about but aware that space was at a premium, he glanced over his shoulder and spoke to Manahan.

"Maybe you'd better wait in the car, Sergeant," he said. "It's a little crowded in here."

"I called you twice," Casey said.

"So I heard," Logan said. "I was busy."

He closed the door behind him, looked for a place to sit

down, and took the chair Delemater had been using. When he was ready he looked at Casey.

"Has this got something to do with homicide?" he demanded.

"Yes," Casey said.

"Whose homicide?" Eagan asked.

"Clem Alpert," Casey said, "and Julius Levy."

He turned and took the strip of film from Delemater and held it up so all could see. He knew what he had to say, but he was a little worried about Logan because the lieutenant had missed the background and he knew he could not go back over it now. Logan was going to be sore, but if things worked out right Logan would get over it. It helped some to remember that he had tried to get Logan earlier and it was not his fault that the lieutenant was late. When he saw the others were waiting, he said:

"This all goes back to Saturday night when Johnny Keeler had his stroke. When I got there he was on the couch unconscious." He glanced at the woman by the window. "Mrs. Jensen was beside him and Clem Alpert was standing in the middle of the room. The door of the darkroom was open, and that never happened unless Keeler was using it. While we waited for the doctor I noticed some things. The safe where he kept his films was unlocked and the keys were in it."

He explained what Alpert had said. "He wouldn't tell me what he and Keeler had been doing; he merely said they had been out together. So Keeler died before morning and I found out that he had left me all his negatives. Julius Levy had sealed them in those two boxes and I left them in his office for the time being. That night Clem Alpert was killed and his office was searched. Lieutenant Logan will tell you that it looked very much as if he had walked in on the person who was doing the searching, had tried to get a gun out of his desk, and was shot. Alpert had a small darkroom and that had been searched, too. The police took the negatives they found, but I haven't heard whether they were of any help or not."

"They weren't," Logan said.

"By that time," Casey continued, "I began to think that

Alpert had taken some films from the safe while Keeler lay unconscious on the floor."

He went on to speak of what had happened in Julius Levy's office the night the lawyer had been fatally slugged. He said the pattern of the crimes suggested that the killer had failed to get what he wanted from Alpert and had continued his search in Levy's office.

"Before Julius Levy was killed," he said, "I did a very bad thing." His glance touched the trio on the davenport without lingering. "I had an offer for some of those negatives, and although I believed what I heard was the truth, I was still worried about my responsibility and I stalled."

He paused as his voice thickened, and the feeling of shame and embarrassment had to be swallowed before he could continue his confession.

"I didn't have guts enough to tell the truth so I said those two boxes of films were still in Levy's filing cabinet. When I went down there two or three hours later and found him on the floor I felt responsible for what had happened. When he died the feeling of guilt got worse."

"Why?" said Logan. "Why should you feel responsible?"

"I thought Levy had been killed because of those films."

"So?"

"Others wanted them," Casey said, making it a point to keep his eyes away from the davenport. "I thought one of them, believing Levy actually did have the negatives, had gone to his office to get them."

"Where were they?"

"In the cellar at my place," Casey said and explained that he had taken the two boxes there earlier. "It wasn't until a couple of hours ago," he added, "that I realized the lie I told had nothing to do with his death. Until then the theory I had been working on was based on the fact that the motive for murder was in those two boxes of films. It wasn't." He again held up the strip of film. "The motive was here all the time."

"So you held out on me again, hunh," Logan said disgustedly.

"I didn't get this film until a couple of hours ago. Sam Dele-mater made prints right here. He only just finished before these gentlemen came. I haven't even had a chance to look at them myself, but I know what's on them."

"Where did you get them?"

"From Fay Novak."

Eagan cleared his throat. "Suppose we let Casey continue, Lieutenant. You can get the details later, can't you?"

Logan, knowing he was licked for the time being, lapsed into a sullen silence and Casey was thankful for the interruption.

"My original theory was a bust," he said. "If I had been real smart, I would have known better when I went into Keeler's darkroom Saturday night." He digressed to describe that darkroom and then said: "There was developer in the thirty-five-millimeter tank. That meant that Keeler had recently developed some film; it also meant he hadn't finished, or at least had just finished, because otherwise he would have dumped out that developer and cleaned the tank. A little heater-fan he used for drying negatives was still on and I turned it off. That, in itself, should have told me that some sort of film had recently been there. The rapid-sequence camera was still on the bench. It was all there," he said morosely, "but I didn't put it together right.

"Oh, I knew he must have just developed some thirty-five-millimeter film," he added quickly, "but I made a very stupid assumption. I thought he had put the film in one of those two boxes that were in the safe. After Keeler had his stroke, I thought Alpert had unlocked the safe and removed the negatives he wanted."

"So what changed your mind?" Logan asked, his resentment still showing.

"Keeler always filed his films individually. I knew that. If he had done it his way, he would have cut the strip into frames. When I saw this four-frame strip a little while ago, I knew it had never been in the safe. It was probably still hanging on that wire with the fan on to dry it."

He paused to glance over the room and the thought came to him that at this point he had more audience than he needed.

"There's no need for you to wait," he said, addressing the men on the davenport. "The negatives you were interested in were old ones. You saw me burn them."

Caldwell and Babcock rose with alacrity. Eagan thought it over and declined the offer.

"If you're going to talk some more about homicide," he said, settling back and crossing his knees, "I might as well stick around. It's going to wind up in my lap eventually anyway."

Casey got hats and coats for the other two, and when he opened the door, Donald Caldwell drew him into the hall.

"I'm sorry I had to lie to the lieutenant about my car the other night," he said with obvious embarrassment. "I was there all right."

"I knew it was your car," Casey said.

"I telephoned Julius Levy after you left my place that night. He said he'd be working in the evening so I went down to ask him to try and put a little pressure on you. I thought maybe he could influence you to agree to our offer. I didn't tell the others but drove down there alone and rode up in the elevator. As I stepped out, I saw a door open farther down the hall. I saw the cleaning woman start to back out of an office, and for some reason I can't explain I didn't want her to see me."

He took a small embarrassed breath and said: "I moved down the side hall to give her a chance to enter another office, and I was still there when the elevator brought you back up and I heard her scream." He gave another faint sigh of regret. "I didn't know what happened, but I guess that scream was too much for me. I didn't know what was going on and I was afraid to find out. I decided I'd better get out of there in a hurry, and when you disappeared in Levy's office I got back into the elevator and started down. . . . I just wanted you to know."

Babcock, who had been standing to one side listening, said:

"That offer we made still goes, Casey. We intended to destroy those films anyway and you did it for us. We'll work it out between us and see that you get a check."

"You can work it out any way you want to," Casey said, "but I don't want the check. Just split it up and see that half of it goes into Keeler's estate—I think the Third National Bank is co-executor. I'd like the other half to go to Alma Jensen."

He stepped back into the room and closed the door before they could reply. He put the strip of film into his pocket and asked Delemater for the prints he had made. He took a quick glance at all four of them and what he saw verified the conclusion he had reached in the studio when he had projected enlargements on white paper. Now he passed two of the prints to Eagan and gave the other two to Logan.

It took the two only a moment to understand what the pictures were all about and, as though by some prearranged signal, their eyes came up and fixed on Stan Garrett. The effect on him was almost instantaneous as he sat upright in his chair, his good-looking face pale, twisted beneath the blond hair.

"It was a frame," he shouted. "A lousy frame."

When no one answered him in the next two or three seconds, John Flynn came out of his chair and walked over to Eagan.

"Could I see those?"

Eagan passed the two prints over and Flynn studied them a moment; then he looked at Garrett, his glance sardonic and accusing.

"So you finally got caught out of school, hunh?" he said as he passed the prints back. "Well, well, well."

"Are you saying that Garrett killed Alpert and Levy?" Logan said.

"Yeah," Casey said.

Delemater, who had been watching the proceedings with alert observing eyes, pushed away from the wall.

"I don't know if it's important," he said calmly, speaking to no one in particular, "but the kid is wearing a piece. I noticed it when he came in."

He started for Garrett as he spoke, his hand darting inside
his coat as the other jumped to his feet. Garrett made a half-
hearted attempt to reach for his hip pocket, but when he saw
he had no chance he looked at Delemater's gun and froze.
Logan, who was caught unaware by the unexpectedness of
Delemater's announcement, came out of his chair and started
forward and Delemater said: "In his hip pocket, Lieutenant."

Garrett made no resistance as Logan expertly spun him
halfway around and lifted the short-barreled revolver from the
pocket. He gave him a sufficient push to tip him back into
the chair. He looked down at the gun in his hand and then at
Casey as Delemater went back and leaned against the wall.

"All right," he said to Casey. "What's the rest of it?"

"I haven't got it all," Casey said.

"You've got a good start."

"I don't know how much you need for an arrest—"

"We'll be the judge of that," Logan said, and Casey looked
at Eagan.

"I don't know how much you need to get an indictment
either."

"Suppose you tell us what you think," Eagan said. "Maybe
we can fill in the gaps."

"You got nothing on me." Garrett repeated his protest. "Not
a thing." He looked at Flynn. "I don't know anything about
any murders."

Flynn's smile was small and fixed as he leaned back in his
chair and lit a cigarette. He said if Garrett was telling the
truth he had nothing to worry about. He said that, speaking
for himself, he wanted to hear what Casey had to say. He said
it might be interesting.

20

THEY WERE all watching Casey as he tried to find the right way to explain the things he had on his mind. To give himself a little more time, he moved over to Eagan and asked to see the two prints he had given him earlier. He did not study them long because he had already made up his mind about the negatives and knew the four exposures were of the same scene and varied only in the position of one subject.

In implication it was a sordid scene but one he knew had been duplicated frequently in New York State, where the only grounds for divorce was adultery. There the stage was set with the connivance of cheap private detectives and small-time divorce lawyers. A divorce having been amicably decided on by the principals, it was then necessary to hire a woman to play the part of corespondent. A hotel or apartment room was usually the background. At a designated time the supposedly injured party would break into the place with a private detective, a camera, and whatever witnesses were needed.

The husband, playing a role he no doubt loathed, was thereby caught in a situation that was sufficiently compromising to justify the complaint of adultery. The whole thing was a travesty, not only on the law but on the people who seriously desired divorce; but until the law was changed, the evidence to satisfy it would be contrived in one way or another.

This was such a picture, but with a difference. The scene was a bedroom. Easily recognizable from the neck up was the woman in the bed with a sheet around her chin. Fay Novak's face was the same in each exposure, but Stan Garrett, clad only in his trousers as he stood near the center of the room, had been caught by the rapid-sequence camera in various attitudes of surprise, confusion, and retreat.

To those in the room the meaning of that picture was obvious. It was, as Garrett had said, a frame. But he had not been a party to that frame. Johnny Keeler had arranged that frame; he had taken the essential photographs and he had hired Clem Alpert, who specialized in such things, to assist him. Alpert, in turn, had employed his former wife to be the third party, and Casey understood why Fay Novak did not want to tell him what was on those films.

"Wouldn't this be sufficient evidence for a divorce?" he asked as he returned the prints to Eagan.

"I'd say so. It still is."

"They framed me," Garrett said hoarsely. "Keeler did it."

"Yes," Casey said. "He didn't like anything about you. He wanted to—"

"He hated my guts."

"—break up your marriage while he could," Casey finished. "He tried before. He told me once he tried to talk some sense into his daughter. He knew you were a chaser, that you were unfaithful whenever you had the chance. Sheila wouldn't listen. I remember how Johnny put it. 'She's got electronic valves in her ears,' he said. 'If I start to say anything bad about Garrett, they close up automatically.' So this time Fay Novak was set up as bait. She did what she had to do to make you think you'd made a conquest and you fell for it."

"She still had her clothes on," Garrett said. "She only took off her dress. They waited until I got my shirt and undershirt off. They had it timed somehow so she popped into bed and pulled the sheet up just as they crashed in and the flashlights started popping. She must have left the door unlocked when we came in."

Casey believed what he had heard and he knew now that everything that had happened since was Johnny Keeler's fault. He was the catalyst who had precipitated the tragedy; this in turn had been compounded because he had died too soon. If he had lived, there would have been no murder. He had his pictures and his evidence; he could have taken the blame for what he had done and for its effect on his daughter and Stanley Garrett. But fate had stepped in to thwart him and death had set the wheels in motion for further violence.

Garrett, who must have known the picture evidence would be shown to his wife, had been given another chance he did not deserve. By getting those films back, he could save a marriage which must then have seemed even more important since his wife would inherit a considerable amount of money, or at least a respectable income for life.

Casey spoke of this now. "Mrs. Jensen knew what Keeler intended to do," he said with a glance at the woman. "So did Julius Levy. They tried to talk him out of it."

"I told him his daughter would never forgive him," Alma Jensen said. "If I could have found those pictures"—she paused to look at Casey, to see if he could now understand why she had tried to steal the two boxes—"I would have destroyed them rather than have her remember her father in that way."

"He knew he'd had a couple of strokes," Casey said and explained to Eagan and Logan what the doctor had said on Saturday night. "If he had lived, there would have been no problem except for Garrett. But Clem Alpert was with him when he processed those films. He was right there on the spot when the attack hit Keeler, and being the kind of guy he was, he took that strip of film. When Keeler died he was in business." He looked at Garrett. "How much did he hit you for?"

"I don't know what you're talking about," he said sullenly. "I know Johnny took the pictures, but that's all I know."

Casey took the strip of film from his pocket along with the envelope with a box number which had been mailed to Fay Novak.

"Alpert played it cagey," he said as he passed over the film and envelope to Logan and Eagan. "He had already mailed these to Fay Novak when Garrett came to the office. He probably called her beforehand and told her what he was doing in case he had trouble getting paid off."

"How did you find her?" Logan said.

The question was unexpected and Casey had to think fast. Because he wanted to do what he could to get the lieutenant back into a more agreeable frame of mind, he gave him a small grin.

"I'm a very popular guy."

"Sure," Logan said dryly.

"I've got friends, spies, pigeons."

"Like Delemater."

"Yeah," Casey said, and explained what had happened at the Davis Street apartment that noon. "Don't forget I tried to get you twice."

"You won't let me forget," Logan said. "Where is she now?"

Casey told him and took time to explain about Dan Hall-mann.

"Alpert didn't die immediately," he said. "He must have told Garrett the films were in the mail. He must have also mentioned Julius Levy in some way. So Garrett went to Fay Novak's apartment, still looking for that envelope, and tried to break in. She pegged a shot through the door to scare him off."

"You got no proof," Garrett said, his voice strained. "No proof at all. You're guessing."

"Certainly I'm guessing," Casey said.

"What did you do with the gun?" Logan asked.

The swift digression seemed to startle Garrett. "What gun?"

"The one you used on Alpert."

"I don't know anything about a gun, but if I had used one, I would have put it somewhere where you'd never find it."

"Sure," Logan said. "Probably in the river."

He had a small notebook in his hand now. It was a loose-leaf affair and he had flipped it open. He was also giving close attention to the revolver he had recently taken from Garrett's hip pocket. What he did then proved to Casey, as he had proved to him so many times before over the years, that Logan had not made homicide lieutenant on luck and personality alone.

"It doesn't matter, Garrett," he said flatly. "This gun is just as good."

Garrett stared at him, furrows gouging his brow and a frightened look showing in his eyes.

"You're out of your mind."

"You took a gun with you when you went to search Alpert's office," Logan continued in the same even tones. "He walked in on you. He tried to get a gun out of his desk and you shot him. But before that I think you searched him, Garrett. You took the gun he was wearing. You got rid of the gun you used on him, but you kept the other one because you still had to find Fay Novak and you thought you might need it."

"No," Garrett said, his voice no more than a whisper.

"Alpert had a pistol permit," Logan said. "Two guns were listed on it. We found the one he pulled on you under his body but the other wasn't in the office; it wasn't in his apartment." He tapped the open notebook with the muzzle of the revolver. "This is the other gun, Garrett. The serial number is on that permit."

He slipped the notebook into his pocket and applied more pressure. "If this is the gun you slugged Levy with—and the medical examiner thinks a gun was used—there's bound to be minute traces of blood or flesh or hair somewhere on it. An expert with a microscope or a spectroscopic analysis can prove it no matter how carefully you wiped it off. I think a judge and jury will be interested to know how and where you got the gun."

Eagan took over as Logan finished. "Make it easy on yourself, Garrett," he said. "We're not trying to prove premeditation."

By now the panic was beginning to show on the man's face. He seemed to be groping for words and, in desperation, turned to Flynn, who had been listening intently and with obvious interest.

"Will you get me a lawyer?"

Flynn shook his head. "Not me, big boy. As of about ten

minutes ago your employment with Flynn Enterprises was terminated. This was your idea. Get your own lawyer."

With the rug so suddenly pulled out from under him, Garrett turned back to Logan, his gaze stricken and his voice reflecting the desperation that had so quickly replaced his defiance.

"He tried to get the gun out of the desk drawer," he said. "He started to point it at me. I had to shoot."

"You had already searched him and taken that gun," Eagan said and indicated the one Logan held.

"Yes."

"What did he tell you before he died?" Logan asked.

"He said he had mailed the films to Fay Novak. He said he had told her if anything happened she was to go to Julius Levy."

"We'll check that with the woman," Logan said. "So what about Levy?"

"I couldn't find Fay Novak," Garrett said. "She didn't come back to her apartment. I thought she might already have gone to see Levy. I had to try and search his office. A couple of minutes more and I would have made it. I didn't mean to kill him," he said, his voice starting to break. "You've got to believe me. I didn't hit him hard. I just wanted to knock him out."

Eagan nodded and stood up. "I guess that's enough for now," he said. "Do you want to take him in, Lieutenant?"

Logan went over to the window and threw it open. He put his fingers between his teeth and whistled for Sergeant Manahan. As he did so, Casey moved to the entryway closet and got his camera. When he had checked the shutter and focus he came back just as Logan was snapping the handcuffs on Garrett.

"Hold it," he said, giving the lieutenant no chance to protest before the flash went off in his face.

Logan blinked. When he could see he scowled at Casey.

"What the hell is that for?"

"You're the arresting officer, aren't you?" Casey said.

"When you see your picture in tomorrow morning's *Express* maybe you'll quit sulking."

Logan tried to maintain the scowl, but he had a little difficulty. It was not easy to stay angry with Casey for very long, and the dark eyes began to reflect the lieutenant's basic good humor. Before he could say anything, Casey put the camera aside and glanced at Flynn and then at Garrett.

"There's just one thing I'd like to get straight," he said and spoke of the private detective named Rogovin. He said he had been worried about Fay Novak and explained how he had told her to go to the Parkview with Dan Hallmann. "Who put Rogovin on me?"

"You can't blame Old Stan for that," Flynn said. "That was my idea. I still wanted those two negatives and I didn't know where you'd put them. Rogovin was tailing you to see if he could catch you with those two boxes under your arm. If that happened and he found out where you took them—"

"Yeah," said Casey. "I get it now. If you knew where they were, you might have tried some more muscle, is that it?"

"I may have had something like that in mind," Flynn said frankly. "I hate to give up on a thing until I know I'm licked."

Sergeant Manahan came in as Flynn got his hat and coat. The two officers went into a brief huddle and started to lead Stan Garrett from the room, and Logan stopped in the doorway long enough to give Casey a long deliberate stare that was somewhat enigmatic but no longer reflected either censure or resentment.

"See me later," he said. "I'll need a statement."

"You'll get it."

"I know I will."

Flynn adjusted his hat when the door closed.

"Thanks for the invitation, Casey," he said. "You put on quite a show. I wouldn't have missed it for the world." He glanced at Eagan. "You won this round, Tim," he said, "thanks to Casey. We'll have at it again on election day."

"That's the way I want it," Eagan said, and when Flynn went out he stepped up to Casey and shook hands. "I appreciate what you did this afternoon and I'm not likely to forget it. Did Caldwell and Babcock say anything to you out there in the hall?"

"Yes," Casey said. "I guess it's all straightened out. They can give you the word."

When Eagan had gone, Casey glanced at Delemater and Alma Jensen and for the first time he could feel his nerves start to relax. The reaction carried over into his mind and the sense of depression he had felt for the last two or three days began to lift. He had no great feeling of satisfaction or ac-complishment for what had happened that afternoon; rather, his over-all reaction was one of relief and it suddenly occurred to him that he had been standing for a long time. His leg muscles were tired, and as the tension lifted, the weariness came. When he thought of an antidote he spoke of it at once.

"I guess we need a drink."

"I'd like one," Alma Jensen said.

"Amen," said Delemater.

"Scotch or bourbon?"

"Scotch, please," the woman said.

"I'll go with you," Delemater said, and once they were in the kitchen and working on the ice tray, he made a suggestion. "That's a lot of woman," he said. "I like big girls; the trouble is they don't always like me. I'll give you a ten per cent dis-count on my bill if you can fix up a date for dinner with me."

Casey peered at him, one brow lifting. "Are you serious?"

"Hell, yes."

"Nothing doing," Casey said and chuckled. "You fix up your own dates. Here, take this drink in to her. I'll give you three minutes to sell her on the idea."

He used up the allotted time by working on his highball and he strengthened it a bit more before he moved back into the living room. The look on Delemater's face was enough to tell him that the proposition had been turned down and Dele-mater promptly confirmed it.

"No discount," he said.

"Too bad. Send me a bill."

"I will."

"And thanks for your help, Sam. I'm sorry you had to miss that sleeper."

"What sleeper?"

"In the tavern this morning you said you thought you had a sleeper at Gulfstream."

"Oh, that one." Delemater's face was suddenly alive again. "I got a small bet down on him while you were talking to Fay Novak, and that reminds me."

He went over to the telephone and dialed a number. He asked his questions and when he hung up and turned a smile was there and he hummed a few bars of some unknown melody.

"He won by three lengths," he said happily. "Paid nine eighty. How about that?" He finished his drink and walked over to the door. "Good-by, Mrs. Jensen," he said. "I hope you meant what you said about some other time because I'm certainly going to give you a ring. . . . See you, Flash," he said without waiting for an answer and then he was gone.

"A great guy." Casey went over and sat down next to the woman. "He likes you."

"I think I like him, too," Alma Jensen said. "And I'm afraid I told him a little fib." She paused to consider Casey's questioning glance and said: "He asked me to have dinner with him. I said maybe some other time. I said you and I had quite a lot to talk about and that I might be having dinner with you." She paused again and now the color was showing in her cheeks. "I'm not usually that forward, and if you're busy—"

The shrill ring of the telephone interrupted her and Casey made muttering sounds as he put aside his glass and went over to it. The voice that came to him was almost incoherent with excitement and it took him a moment to understand that it was Dan Hallmann who had called.

"The police were here. They took Fay to headquarters. They wouldn't let me go with her. I want to get a lawyer. Do you know a good one, Mr. Casey?"

Casey spoke bluntly, telling Hallmann to calm down. He

said to take it easy, that there was nothing to worry about.

"They just want to question her," he said.

"But how long will they keep her?"

"Probably not more than a couple of hours."

"We had a long talk this afternoon," Hallmann said, distress still warping his phrases. "She told me everything, Mr. Casey, and it doesn't matter a bit. Are you sure she's not in some bad trouble?"

"Positive," Casey said.

"Then what should I do?"

"Stay right where you are," Casey said. "If you get hungry, have something sent up to your room. When they finish questioning her, she's sure to come back to you so just keep your fingers crossed and sweat it out. I'll tell you what I'll do. Maybe later I can stop by and we'll have a drink."

"Would you?"

"I will if I can," Casey said. "Just take it easy."

He hung up and let his breath out in a long audible gust. He shook his head and told Alma Jensen what had happened, not seeing the odd softness that began to grow in her green eyes or quite understanding what she meant when she said:

"That was an awfully nice thing to do."

"Ahh—" It was a deprecating sound accompanied by a shrug. "The poor guy's out of his mind. He's nuts about Fay and I'm glad she's getting a break. . . . Now about this dinner business."

He stopped in front of her and looked down, his dark eyes amused and definitely interested. He found the suggestion that had been made both flattering and apropos, and he was reminded again that this was not only a very handsome woman but the sort of company that was not always easy to find. He was also aware that, after what had happened today, this was not an evening when a man should be alone.

"You have got yourself a date, Alma," he said. "We do have some things to talk about, don't we? I'll tell you what. I've got to get this picture back to the studio. If you don't mind waiting a few minutes, you can go with me. I want to clean up a bit, and after we've been to the office we can have a drink or two and decide where we want to eat."

Alma Jensen smiled up at him, her eyes content and her mouth curving softly. She said she would wait, and Casey gave her a small salute of acknowledgement. By the time he had moved into the bedroom and closed the door, his grin, though unconscious, was constant. He began to whistle softly as he started to change his clothes.

A NOTE ON THE TYPE

The text of this book is set in Caledonia, a Linotype face designed by W. A. Dwiggins, the man responsible for so much that is good in contemporary book design and typography. Caledonia belongs to the family of printing types called "modern face" by printers—a term used to mark the change in style of type-letters that occurred about 1800. Caledonia borders on the general design of Scotch Modern but is more freely drawn than that letter.

A NOTE ABOUT THE AUTHOR

GEORGE HARMON COXE *was born in Olean, New York, and spent his youth there and in nearby Elmira. After a year at Purdue and one at Cornell, he worked for five years on newspapers in California, Florida, and New York, and did advertising for a New England printer for five years more. Since that time he has devoted himself to writing—for two years with Metro-Goldwyn-Mayer, then as a free lance, selling numerous short stories, novelettes, and serials to magazines as well as to motion-picture, radio, and television producers.*

He is a past president of the Mystery Writers of America.

JANUARY 1962